FOUL RISING

An Elmwood Mystery

Mark H. Bliss

Foul Rising

Copyright 2021 by Mark H. Bliss

mbliss3901@yahoo.com

facebook.com/markhbliss15

First Edition

Acknowledgements

This book is dedicated to my wife Marcia, whose editing skills and sage advice greatly enhanced the writing. I also want to thank fellow author and former journalist Jim Wilder for his immense help in navigating me through the intricacies of book publishing and encouraging me every step of the way. I also wish to thank fellow writer and former journalist Marybeth Niederkorn for reading the manuscript and offering both advice and encouragement. My novel also benefits from the expertise of Dave Lappin, who designed the book cover and layout. This novel owes a great deal to my lengthy career in journalism, which gave me the opportunity to report on the life of a Mississippi River community and its people, and to share a newsroom with talented folks at every level, from publishers to editors and reporters to photographers. Lastly, living in a Mississippi River town has given me a daily appreciation of this waterway and its immense power to shape lives and the communities it touches.

The Mississippi River will always have its own way; no engineering skill can persuade it to do otherwise.

-- Mark Twain

Prologue

1995

Hamilton Jones stood on his rotting wood porch, careful not to tread on the worst planks, and stared at the inky night sky.

In the distance gleamed the lights of the city, Elmwood, perched on the Missouri side of the Mighty Mississippi, above a concrete floodwall. At night, the wall appeared like a brooding gray wash on the landscape.

Jones didn't care much for the town. Too snooty for him. He preferred cricket serenades and the moist earth of Southern Illinois. Cleared of swamp trees, the land nurtured soybeans and corn.

Some farmers were rich. But most farms were small, little more than a few hundred acres. What wasn't farmed was swamp land: muck, mud and rotting trees. The few towns were barely more than rusted out trailer parks and run-down bars whose concrete block walls seemed to sink into their marshy surroundings.

Jones preferred his own company to those of others. At age 90, he was no longer able to farm his own land. He leased the 300 acres to a neighboring and younger farmer who plowed the fields and grew the corn and soybeans. But he still owned the family farm his ancestors had worked for more than a century and lived in the two-story weathered farmhouse where he was born.

His wife Edna had died five years earlier. They had no children. He was all alone now, except for a few nieces and nephews, who seldom stopped by.

With his long white hair, dressed in jeans and long-sleeved flannel shirt, Jones looked more like a country singer than a farmer. But he couldn't play a lick. Seldom listened to the radio. He preferred the sounds of nature, the birds cawing and the coyotes moaning.

Jones glanced once more at the darkness. He knew the raging

1

river. Spring flooding. But the earthen levee on his side of the river was holding, at least for now. He wasn't worried. He had survived past floods, including '73 and '93 when the river had drowned whole communities.

In '93, the wild river gouged a hole in his earthen farm levee. The raging water rushed over his fields. Muddy water tore up his wooden front steps and climbed into his first floor, tearing away at the wood frame walls and the pine-plank floor. But he survived and repaired the damaged home to some extent. Enough to make it livable.

It was never a show home. He was fine with that. It was well worn and so was he.

Now, standing on his porch, he was surrounded by mosquitoes. "Damn blood suckers," he said, swatting at the irritating insects. He let out a sigh and went inside. Time for bed.

He awoke hours later to a strange, rushing sound. The boards in the house groaned like a wounded animal. Jones staggered out of bed. Maybe it was the bourbon, he thought. He regularly downed Wild Turkey before bed.

Slowly, he walked to the front door, dressed in well-worn PJs. He opened the oak door. The night sky blurred amid an avalanche of mud and murky water. It punched him in the gut, sending him staggering inside. It crushed him against the living room wall, spanking him with floundering fish. The water launched tree limbs at his body, cutting him.

The river was filling up his house. He tried to reach the stairway to climb to the second floor, but floodwaters toppled his massive, 1850s-era desk on top of him, crushing his lungs. He was on the floor now, struggling to breathe. He gulped; muddy water washed inside him. He was drowning. He tried to call out, but there was no sound. Trapped under water, he was losing consciousness.

The last thing he remembered was a small fish flushed into his mouth from the raging water; scaly, muddy death concealed in darkness and debris.

CHAPTER ONE

2018

A wry smile creased the face of Connor Tate as he scribbled down the mayor's remarks in a reporter's notebook.

Mayor Elroy James spoke to a small crowd, comprised mostly of city and civic leaders, proclaiming the importance of a new steel sculpture erected in the middle of downtown Elmwood as dark clouds gathered above.

It was going to storm soon. Another deluge. Rain had been a constant companion for more than a month. Still, the threat of more rain had not dampened the mayor's enthusiasm for the new sculpture and an opportunity to give another speech.

"This piece will welcome visitors to our historic downtown and show everyone that we are a progressive community that values the arts," Elroy said, looking down from a bucket truck and hoping he wouldn't get struck by lightning. With that, he pulled a rope, causing a curtain hiding the sculpture to fall to the ground.

Connor eyed the 14-foot jagged sculpture. It reminded him more of a middle-finger, fuck-off gesture than anything else.

But to Elroy, it was a fabulous work of art. In his four years in office, he had succeeded in having artists install metal sculptures all along downtown streets. He wasn't about to let this roundabout escape a sculpture.

Local college art professor Randy Wright had fashioned the latest sculpture with the help of his students. "I call it, 'Contemplation,'" he proudly told Connor, who was thinking to himself, "what a bunch of crap."

Elroy, having descended from the bucket truck, approached.

"Hi, Connor. What do you think of our new sculpture? Isn't it great?"

"Well, it definitely will be noticed," Connor answered.

"One of these days, you'll appreciate all this artwork," Elroy said, laughing, before turning to shake hands with Chamber of Commerce leaders.

Connor doubted he would ever appreciate the sculptures around town, some of which resembled giant, rusty Tinker Toys to him.

"At least, it made for a good photo," Tyler Frazier told him. Dressed in jeans, orange tennis shoes and a green flannel shirt, Tyler was one of three photographers at the River City Journal where Connor worked.

Connor liked Tyler. He was talented. Tyler had been at the paper for about a year. Probably wouldn't stay much longer, Connor figured. The daily newspaper in Elmwood was known for losing talented employees to higher paying journalism jobs elsewhere.

At age 50, Connor was nearly 30 years older than Tyler. He had worked at the River City Journal most of his adult life. He had raised two daughters and gone through two marriages. Too much drinking and time spent covering lying politicians and investigating wrongdoing.

He loved the newsroom, the late-night deadlines, even the smell of newsprint. It was intoxicating. The pay – not so much. It was a family owned newspaper and the publisher was a tight wad. The money stayed in the family. To the publisher's way of thinking, reporters could be replaced, and he would save money.

Connor was not a fancy dresser. His standard attire was gray jeans, plaid shirts and black dress shoes. Raised in St. Louis, he was a city boy. He said he was "ruralized" living in Elmwood, a city of about 40,000 people perched beside the Mississippi River.

But he liked the 10-minute commute from his home on the western edge of the city. Having a college helped too. It brought concerts and diverse opinions to the hilly community. There were plenty of restaurants too, which Connor appreciated. He didn't like to cook, not when he could have a shrimp po-boy and a draft beer at the polished wooden bar in the downtown Cajun restaurant.

Founded by French fur traders in the late 1700s, Elmwood was platted as a town in the early 1800s. It was named for the forest of elms that once populated the landscape.

In the 1850s, Andrew Ramsey a descendant of one of the town's founding families, built a plantation style mansion on a bluff overlooking the downtown. Aging elms lined the entrance to the property.

4

The mansion was no longer a home, having been converted into a regional history museum in 1990. The elms were gone, victims of Dutch Elm disease. But residents still took pride in the imposing brick structure with its massive white columns and wide front porch. The fact that the home was built by and serviced by slaves was an inconvenient truth that most residents and city leaders chose to ignore.

The newspaper, established in 1900, was located in one of the city's historic buildings, and only a short walk from one of Connor's favorite drinking establishments.

Connor particularly liked investigating corrupt cops. And there were a lot of them in Southeast Missouri. His efforts recently had helped secure freedom for an innocent man, who had spent 17 years behind bars for a murder he didn't commit. Cops, in that case, intimidated witnesses and conspired to pin the murder of a woman on the man, knowing he was not the shooter, but wanting this African American male off the streets because of his past criminal record.

Exposing corrupt cops was exciting. Covering the unveiling of an ugly sculpture was not thrilling, but it had to be done.

Connor made a mental note to check on how much this sculpture was costing city taxpayers. City officials were talking about the need for a sales tax to better fund the police department even as the mayor championed spending tax dollars on public art.

Connor took in the scene around the horrible sculpture as the wind picked up. The smell of rain was in the air. A crowd still milled around the steel creation, ignoring the impending weather. Civic leaders congratulated the mayor even though many of them would have objected to having the same pile of steel placed in their front yards. "Hypocrites," Connor thought.

Not everyone was focused on the sculpture. A tall, thin man stood at the back of the crowd. His long, slightly graying hair showed from beneath a red baseball cap.

His dark eyes stared down the street. Two blocks away, at the river's edge, towered the concrete monster. He wished he could slay it, return things to the natural order. He dreamed of the wall crumbling, the swollen river rushing in and drowning everything in its path. He smiled at the thought as he turned his back on the crowd and walked away. As for the sculpture, the art was shit, he thought. It could drown too.

CHAPTER TWO

As the sculpture was unveiled, two blocks away, city crews were closing the massive, steel floodgate amid angry skies.

Elmwood public works director Clay Smith looked on with a sense of unease. Floodwaters had nearly topped the floodwall in 2011 before the Army Corps of Engineers had ignited liquid explosives, blowing huge holes in a Bootheel earthen levee 45 miles south of the city, flooding valuable farmland and generating anger among those affected farmers, but relief for the citizens of Elmwood and those communities across the river in Illinois.

The Elmwood floodwall was in need of major repairs, Corps officials warned city leaders last year. But Congress had yet to appropriate federal funds to shore up the wall. This time, he felt sure, the Corps would not blow any holes in an agricultural levee to save the city. Elmwood was on its own.

Floodwaters were already racing and swirling down river, fueled by weeks of melting snow and heavy rains in the Upper Midwest. Elmwood had seen little snow this winter, but it had received tons of rain.

Now entering March, the forecast called for more rain. The forecast was getting tedious and worrisome.

As the steel floodgate was being closed and anchored shut, the muddy water already had climbed the tiered, concrete riverfront plaza on the river side of the floodwall. Water was within two feet of the gate.

The 20-foot high wall was built atop the crest of the riverbank. Engineers estimated floodwaters would have to reach 52 feet on the river gauge to overtop the levee and turn the downtown into a lake. But in 2011, the river came close, reaching 50 feet for the first time ever.

When the river was not at flood stage, the gate was kept open, allowing residents and visitors alike to stand on the shore and watch the river flowing unceasingly toward New Orleans.

Passenger boats, designed as paddle wheelers, made regular stops in Elmwood on trips up and down the Mighty Mississippi. But at times like this, the floodgate closed off the river view and the concrete barrier became a sort of castle wall, designed to protect its citizens from a watery invasion.

The Corps in recent years had made some minor repairs to the levee, but more work was needed to shore up the concrete foundation.

Smith worried that a more than 50-year-old wall might not withstand another onslaught from Ole Man River.

He tried to ignore the worries as he assisted his crew in stacking sandbags against the now closed floodgate. While the gate helped hold back the waters, some water still seeped under the gate. The sandbags helped keep the seepage to a minimum.

"Good job, guys," Smith said as the workers climbed back into white, city public works trucks. Their job was done for now. But soon, he knew, floodwaters would lay siege to the city, pressing up against the wall like a mighty army.

Two blocks west, Connor finished scribbling in his notebook, having interviewed all of the notable officials in attendance at the unveiling of the sculpture.

He headed to his red Ford Escape, in a hurry to get back to the office and crank out the story. He had a more important task on his mind, tracking down more witnesses to a timecard fraud scheme involving a police chief and his son in a nearby town.

He had already written two stories on then case, which prompted the town's mayor, who rode around in a pickup truck sporting a huge Trump sign, to cuss him out and accuse him of creating "fake news."

Never mind that the police chief had forged his son's name on a timecard so his son could get paid even though he wasn't doing his police job. Residents said they never saw the son, and most didn't even know he was a cop.

He only showed up at high school basketball games to ogle the cheerleaders. The police chief said his son was doing undercover work most nights, although no one had been arrested in the town of 200 people for more than a year now.

Connor reached his parked SUV. As he unlocked the door, he

saw a thin piece of paper had been wedged under his windshield wiper. He pulled it out. Typed on the paper was a brief message, "Nahum, 1:8. DROWNING, DROWNING, DROWN."

Connor crumpled the strip of paper and threw it on the passenger side floor. Connor had never heard of Nahum. Was it a book of the Bible? And what's this stuff about drowning? A cry for help or a silly threat?

Maybe the message was left there by some Mormon missionary, he reasoned. He scanned the horizon, looking for a white-shirted man on a bike, but saw no one fitting that description.

He drove the five blocks back to the paper, his mind dismissing what he viewed as nothing but gibberish.

Back in the newsroom, he set to work crafting the story of the hideous sculpture, trying not to let his feelings shape the story.

The newspaper was located in a sprawling, two-story brick building that looked more like a warehouse than an office building. Founded in 1904, the River City Journal looked out over the downtown and the nearby historic courthouse.

The newsroom was located in the rear of the building. It had high ceilings as a result of having housed the newspaper presses for years. The presses were later moved to a separate building a few blocks away.

Connor finished his story and marked it ready to edit. He looked up to see his editor approaching his cluttered desk. "Will I be admonished for not cleaning up my desk again?" wondered Connor, who was skeptical of anyone with a clean desk. "If it's clean, it means someone isn't doing his or her job," he often told colleagues.

Editor Dave Lansmon was a large, balding man with a gruff demeanor. But behind that exterior was a man who generally felt kindly about his reporters, copy desk editors, and the photographers. He would fight for the newsroom and often did when the publisher upstairs talked of wanting to cut the reporting budget.

Connor was older than Lansmon, who had been hired as editor about 15 years ago.

Both men shared one thing in common: they loved investigative journalism, which often put them at odds with the publisher who favored stories about new restaurants over articles about public corruption.

Lansmon carried a cardboard box to Connor's desk. He turned it over and two dozen strips of paper fluttered onto the desk. Connor gazed at them, noting all contained, typed letters and numbers, and the "drowning" words. The words with the numbers were brief: Genesis, Daniel, Amos, Joshua and Job, among others.

"These messages have been found on the parked vehicles of Elmwood City Council members, including the mayor, and chamber leaders," Lansmon said. "Find out what's going on. Is this the work of some religious nut? Can someone be arrested for this nonsense?"

"I got one of these myself," Connor said.

"Well, maybe you can uncover who is behind this nuisance and why anyone would want to dump Bible verses all over town," Lansmon said.

"I'm on it. It's probably just a stupid prank. Maybe the police will know something."

"Don't count on it. Police officers here seem to look the other way when it comes to most nuisance complaints and I doubt such messages are mentioned in the city's nuisance ordinance.

"You mean the one about the dogs and cats living together," Connor joked.

"Yeah. That one." Lansmon laughed.

CHAPTER THREE

Connor picked up the phone and called his friend, police detective Adam Dade.

"What's happening, Connor?" Adam asked.

"I am looking into these Bible verses flooding the area. You heard about them?"

"Yeah. Been looking into them for the past several hours, ever since the mayor first called the police chief earlier this morning. Elroy seems traumatized by the whole thing. Personally, I don't know if it will amount to much."

"I checked some of the references. They are all deal with flooding," Connor said, adding that he, too; had received a Bible verse.

"I know," replied Adam. "One of the verses says, 'with an overrunning flood he will make an utter end of the place thereof, and darkness shall pursue his enemies.'"

"Sounds like someone hopes for some major flood damage," Connor suggested.

"Could be. But if that's the case, it's some sick individual," Adam said.

"Is it illegal to spread Bible verses all over town? Is it littering?"

"We've checked with the city attorney. He said you could make a nuisance case, but it is pretty thin. It's not like KKK hate messages. It's the Bible. A lot of folks here would not take kindly to prosecuting someone for preaching God's word."

"That's assuming it's God's will." Connor replied. "Bible verses are one thing but littering them everywhere is something else. Has anyone seen someone placing these verses on car windshields?"

"Haven't found anyone yet. But we put a post on Facebook. Maybe someone will call in. I will let you know if we find out anything, but I wouldn't get your hopes up. These days, we are more worried about drive-by shootings than verse-filled scraps of paper."

Connor hung up. Seemed to be a dead end so far.

He phoned the mayor. Elroy picked up on the first ring. "Hi,

Connor," he said.

"Hey, Mayor. Wanted to ask you about those Bible verses. I understand that you and other council members found them on your cars."

"Yes, when we returned to our cars after the sculpture dedication. It was strange. None of us knew what to make of it. We googled the messages, found out they referenced Bible verses about flooding."

"I spoke to the police. They say you're upset about it."

"Not just me," he exclaimed. "The city manager, the chamber president, we all are upset. People are on edge because of all the flooding up and down the river. Without the floodwall, this town would be wiped out."

"Well, the downtown for sure," Connor said.

"Without the downtown, we don't have a city. The city's origins are tied to the river, this nation's first superhighway. It is the life-blood of our community."

"You think whoever distributed those verses is threatening the city?" Connor asked.

"Could be. But, if so, that person is making a serious mistake. Our police department will get to the bottom of it, I promise you that. I got to go. Nice talking to you," Elroy said, hanging up.

Then the rains came. It rained off and on, mostly on, for the next eight days. Streets turned into rivers, car tires spraying water everywhere including on umbrella-carrying pedestrians trying to navigate the sidewalks.

By mid-March, it had turned sunny, but cool for spring. But the river was still rising, now at 42 feet, with no end in sight.

No more Bible verses had been found, but that didn't settle down city leaders, who prayed the floodwall would hold.

Connor had uncovered a Corps of Engineers report from two years earlier that had concluded there was a risk, even with repairs, that the floodwall would not hold up to a 100-year flood, the kind that had been happening almost yearly for the past seven years.

The newspaper published the story, angering already upset city officials.

Adam called on a Wednesday morning. He made no mention of city officials' anger. "Got some news about those Bible verses. We think we may know who distributed them."

"Who?"

"A bartender at Alligator Alley," said Adam, referring to a downtown Cajun restaurant and popular drinking establishment on Main Street. "I am going to go talk to the bartender now. Want to tag along?"

"Sure. I will meet you there."

Billy Moss poured a Blue Moon draft for a customer at the bar, who apparently was getting a head start on a liquid lunch, just as the front door opened. Connor and Adam walked in.

"What will you have, guys?" Billy asked.

"Information," said the detective who showed up in coat and tie, dress slacks and polished black shoes. By contrast, Connor looked like a slob in his worn jeans, old sweatshirt and scuffed tennis shoes.

"What kind of information?" asked Billy, his eyes narrowing with suspicion.

"The kind that might keep you out of jail," replied Adam.

Billy swallowed hard and looked questioningly at Adam and then Connor.

"Well, I will be glad to help. What is this all about."

"It's about Bible verses," Connor said, receiving a hard stare from Adam who had previously stressed to Connor he would ask the questions.

"We have a witness who says he saw you put those verses on car windshields," Adam said bluntly.

"Damn. I knew it was too good to be true."

"What was?" asked Adam.

"I figured it was just a way to make some extra money?"

"How?"

"About a month ago, someone left a note at the bar. It was a busy Friday night. The bar was full. I didn't see who left the note."

"Who was the note addressed to?"

"It was addressed to me."

"What did it say?"

"It said I could make $5,000 if I planted certain Bible verses on particular cars. I was told to leave a note taped to a downtown trash can if I was interested."

"So, you did that?"

"Yes. A couple days later I found another unsigned note at the bar. It was a list of verse numbers from the Bible and the drowning message. The note instructed me to type each one on strips of paper. It also told me where to find the cars on which to place the messages. I placed a bunch of them on cars parked by the roundabout, when city leaders were dedicating that sculpture."

"So, you have no clue who wrote the note?"

"No. I told you I never saw who put the note on the bar."

"Did you get paid?"

"Yes, I arrived at work one night and found a blank envelope sitting on the far edge of the bar, under a stack of coasters."

"How did you know it was for you?" Adam asked.

"Because it had $5,000 cash in it, all of it in $20 bills. Nobody would leave a tip like that."

"Do you still have the notes?"

"No, I shredded them."

"Why did you do that?" asked Adam, dismayed by the answer.

"I didn't want my boss to find out. I thought he might think I was taking a bribe or something. After I did it, I was worried that I might have done something illegal."

"Well, you've upset a lot of people. Bible verses about flooding are no laughing matter in the midst of river flooding," Adam said. "I will get back to you once I have talked to the police chief. Meanwhile, if you remember anything else, call me right away. Do I make myself clear?"

"Yes," Billy said softly, an embarrassed look on his face. "I didn't mean any harm. Honest."

Adam and Connor stepped outside.

"What do you think?" Adam asked Connor.

"I think he might be telling the truth. It is too stupid a story not to be true."

"I agree. He's a 20-something who is probably earning dirt wages. He sees a chance to make a little extra money."

"But if that is the case," Connor began, "then this case is far from solved."

"You're right. Whoever orchestrated this thing had a reason. We don't know what that reason is. And not knowing makes me nervous. I hope we find this guy and soon."

CHAPTER FOUR

Dressed all in black, the man worked hurriedly, painting blood-red words on a section of the floodwall, defacing the floodwall mural.

The paint dripped, just like blood. The 3-foot-tall words spread out over about 20 feet of wall. "DIE ELMWOOD DIE."

He felt anxious and excited at the same time. On the other side of the floodwall, the water was pressing in, plunging away at cracks in the aging concrete. Everyone knew the wall needed repairs. It was still holding up, but for how long. Not for long if he had his way.

The man stepped back from the wall and gazed at his creation. He smiled with satisfaction, imagining the next story in the newspaper, full of comments from frustrated and worried city leaders.

He felt the power that comes with controlling the narrative. He looked around to make sure he was alone. It was 3 a.m., no moon. There were downtown streetlights, but this section of the floodwall veered farther away from River Street. He was in the shadows.

He closed the lid of the paint can, grabbed the handle of the can and his paint brush and began walking up the hill, back to his car parked three blocks away in an unlit alley.

He was halfway there when he spotted the pedestrian. He knew instantly who it was. He knew the other man's gait. The way he held his head and shuffled his arms at the end of his shift.

It was Billy Moss. The bartender was probably on his way back to his downtown loft apartment. The black-clad man knew Moss often stayed at work long after the bar closed. Moss liked to play music on the antique jukebox and dream a bit. Moss also liked to pour himself a few cold ones, on the house so to speak.

Moss saw the man carrying the paint brush and can. What's a painter doing out at this hour? Maybe this guy is just drunk. But the man wasn't staggering. Moss saw the man turn toward him briefly and then hurry down a side street.

Moss shook his head. You never knew what you might see

14

downtown. He recalled once seeing a naked woman, big breasted, riding her bike past Alligator Alley as he was closing up. She had peacock feathers in her hair and seemed oblivious to his wide-eyed stares.

Still, this felt different. More sinister somehow. He kept walking, heading home.

The man in black walked up one street and down another, turning left on a side street and then right at another, over and over. He wanted to make sure Moss wasn't following him.

Finally satisfied, he found his SUV unlocked it and slipped inside, placing the paint can and the brush into a black, plastic garbage bag on the front, passenger-side floor.

He was safe for now. But he creased his brow, worried that the bartender might talk to the police. He had eaten at the restaurant numerous times in the past although he never sat at the bar or talked directly to Moss.

Still, it was a risk, made worse by the fact it's not normal to see a man walking downtown with a paint can at 3 a.m. So, he would have to think about it. Maybe he should eliminate the risk. How? When? Where? Those were the questions crossing his mind, over and over.

When he arrived home, he decided to sleep on it, glad he lived alone and had no one to whom he had to explain his comings and goings.

By the time he woke up later that morning, his message was all over the news.

***

Connor zipped up his jacket in the cool morning breeze as he watched uniformed police and suit-coated detectives examine the painted threat on the floodwall.

Adam saw Connor and walked over to him.

"Kind of early for you," he said.

Connor looked at his watch. It was 8 a.m. Connor didn't usually start his day until about 9 o'clock.

"Yeah, well I was just getting out of the shower when my editor called. What do you know about this graffiti?"

"Not much," replied Adam. "A city worker driving the street

sweeper reported it. The tech guys say they haven't found any fin-gerprints. The perpetrator probably wore gloves."

"Any clues?"

"Found a partial shoe print. Looks like a tennis shoe. Tons of people wear such shoes. Doubt that will be much help," Adam said.

"You think this is related to the Bible verses about flooding?" Connor asked.

"Possibly. But it could be unrelated. Just some kids who thought it would be fun to deface the floodwall."

"True. But regardless, city officials are going to go crazy over this. Probably issue a news release. Maybe even offer a reward for information leading to an arrest."

"Yeah, well, I will let you know if we find out anything else we can disclose to the media," said Adam before heading back to the vandalized wall and away from television reporters who were clustered together, their videographers recording the actions of the police investigating the vandalism.

Adam turned to see Police Chief Blair Bonney walking toward the reporters. Bonney loved being in front of the camera. There wasn't much to tell, but Adam knew the chief would tell it with gusto.

Connor sighed as he walked over to the gaggle of reporters. He was ready to quote Bonney, if nothing else because Lansmon would want a quote from the chief or "Bare Bones" as reporters called him behind his back. The nickname referenced the chief's standard reply to questions from the media. "I will give you just the facts, nothing more," he would state.

After the chief's impromptu news conference, Connor returned to the newsroom where he met up with Tyler who had photographed the scene.

Lansmon joined the two men.

"Well, what have we got?"

"Good art," said Tyler. "Front page art."

"Alright, we've got the photo. What about the story?" asked Lansmon, turning to Connor.

"Not much yet. Could be tied to the Bible verses. Cops aren't sure."

"Well, focus the story on the continued flooding. Wrap the

floodwall vandalism into the overall flood story for now," Lansmon ordered.

"Sounds good," Connor replied and headed back to his messy desk.

He pulled up the National Weather Service regional office home page on his computer. The river stage was approaching 45 feet. It was still rising. About 100 miles to the north, the raging Missouri River dumped into the Mississippi, fueling the flooding even more.

All that water was headed downstream, toward Elmwood. Connor knew the flooding would get worse.

Connor's phone rang. It was the mayor. "Did you see all the damage?" Elroy asked.

"Yes."

"It wrecked the mural. That mural is a tourist attraction. Now, the city will have to spend tax dollars to repair it."

Five years earlier, the City Council hired an artist from Dallas, Texas, to portray the city's history on the city side of the floodwall.

The mural consisted of 24 large, brightly painted panels, depicting everything from the city's founding to its steamboat and Civil War heritage and its later years, culminating with the opening of its new cable-stay bridge, which connected Elmwood on the Missouri side to East Elmwood on the Illinois side.

"Fixing it won't be cheap," lamented Elroy.

"But at least it can be fixed," Connor replied.

"Yeah, but right now it's a damn mess," Elroy said before hanging up.

Connor spent the rest of the morning at his desk, making calls to the Corps of Engineers, the Weather Service, and local emergency management and public works officials to find out the latest news on the flood flight.

By early afternoon, he had written the flood story. He could add to it later.

Connor sat at his desk, his right hand squeezing a gray stress ball, a souvenir from a chamber dinner.

"A penny for your thoughts," said Rachel Short, who was anything, but that. Short had long legs and long auburn hair. She was wearing black jeans, a white, long-sleeved shirt that tightly fitted her torso and black boots.

Short, who was 35, had worked at the paper for about two years, joining the newsroom after a dozen years working at various weekly papers in the Bootheel. She covered the education beat and sat at a desk in the cubicle next to Connor's.

"I can't seem to get a handle on this graffiti story. The message appears to be a threat tied to the floodwall. But why would anyone want to damage a floodwall."

"Perhaps, that should be the focus of your story," replied Rachel, whose hazel eyes smiled at him. "Find out the history of the floodwall and see if anyone locally has opposed such structures."

"Good idea. You may be on to something," he told her.

He watched her walk back to her desk. He was more than a dozen years her senior, but he liked her company. He wondered if she would say yes, if he asked her out. She didn't have a regular boyfriend, though he knew she had dates. She was a regular at several downtown bars. Nothing serious, he thought. But he would love to spend time with her, see where it led. He wasn't looking for a bride, he mused, just a friend with benefits. Maybe, just maybe, he had a future with her.

CHAPTER FIVE

Henry Carter greeted Connor at the front entrance to Elmwood Mansion, now the city's regional history museum.

Connor had phoned ahead. Henry was expecting him.

"So, you want to know a little history about the floodwall?" he asked. "Does your interest have anything to do with the nasty message found on the wall?"

"Yes. I am trying to discern why anyone would have such a hatred of the wall."

"Well, I will see if I can help. Follow me."

Henry, dressed in his favorite plaid sports coat, brown pants, white dress shirt and blue bowtie, led Connor through the ornate first floor to a less elegant room in the back of the mansion, a room that originally served as the maid quarters. Now it served as Henry's office.

A college history professor emeritus, the 70-year-old Henry had retired into a new job as curator of the museum a decade ago. He was a walking encyclopedia of the storied history of Elmwood and the heritage of the entire region.

Henry opened a drawer in an old wooden cabinet and pulled out a large album full of catalogued photos, accompanied by a computer printout of information about the floodwall and flooding in Elmwood dating back to the 1900s.

He carefully removed several black and white pictures showing downtown floods in the 1930s and 1940s.

"The downtown used to flood every year in the spring. There was no floodwall. The Mississippi River turned downtown into a lake. People had to boat to get to their stores. Some of the old brick buildings fronting River Street date back to the 1840s. They were built as warehouses to serve the steamboats that stopped here. They were designed to withstand the flooding. Their ground floors were sloped toward the front so the water would drain as the river level receded."

"So, when did the community start thinking about building a floodwall?"

"In the 1930s. Horrendous flooding up and down the river in 1927 led local and federal officials to begin looking at ways to lessen flood damage. Their solution was to construct countless floodwalls and earthen levees up and down the river. But nothing moves fast with the federal government. It doesn't now and it didn't then. World War II intervened and it took until the 1950s and the Eisenhower administration before federal funding was secured to build the wall."

"So, when did they start building the wall?" Connor asked.

"Construction began in 1956 and ended in 1964 at a cost of more than $4 million," Henry said, pulling out black and white photos from protected sleeves, showing some of the early construction work.

"It would probably cost hundreds of millions of dollars to construct something similar today," Connor suggested.

"Very true. The reinforced concrete wall stretches more than 6,200 feet and is flanked on the north end by a dirt levee."

"Why was there no dirt levee on the south end?"

"I'd credit it to racism. Blacks lived in what was shantytown, an area of rundown shacks and dirt roads that hugged the low-lying area bordering the river. The white merchants and city leaders didn't see a need to protect the dilapidated area. Most blacks didn't vote. City leaders saw no political reason to protect the black neighborhood. In fact, I'm sure they paid little attention to Elmwood's black residents, who mostly worked as maids and laborers. Even the newspaper seldom carried articles about the black residents. Their deaths went unreported. To the white community, black residents were largely invisible."

"That's a sad chapter in this community's history," Connor observed, his attention suddenly focused on a black and white image of a man standing on a ladder in the middle of Main Street. Information attached to the photo indicated it was taken in June 1953.

"Who is that man?"

"It's Wyatt Moss. He was mayor of Elmwood at the time and one of the loudest proponents of the floodwall. He was holding a downtown rally in support of a floodwall when this photo was snapped," Henry explained.

"Moss. Is Billy Moss related to this guy?"

"Yes. Wyatt was Billy's great-grandfather."

"I can see the family resemblance. I didn't know Billy had such a connection to the floodwall."

"Yes. So much of Elmwood's history is family history."

"But in terms of the floodwall today, can you think of anyone who would want to destroy it? It seems like such a part of the city today. I can't see anyone wanting to level it, not with the seemingly worse flooding every year."

"Well, there are those environmentalists who view all flood-walls as bad," observed Henry. "I recall one of the local college professors wrote a piece in the campus newspaper about five years ago in which he argued floodwalls only make the flooding worse."

"You remember his name?"

"No, but I am sure you could find the story in the paper's archive on its website."

"I'll do that. Thanks," Connor replied as he headed for the door.

Could there be a crazed environmentalist out there who wanted to bring down the wall? Or just someone who wanted to draw attention to a cause? Connor had lots of questions, but no answers.

Back in the newsroom, Connor checked the website of the Campus Caller, the weekly student newspaper at Elmwood College.

He clicked on the Archives and searched for the opinion piece. He soon found it. It was titled: "The Problem with Floodwalls." It was written by environmental science professor Tanner Holloway.

Connor looked up Holloway's contact number and email address on the college's website. He knew from experience that college professors often didn't answer their office phones. He emailed Dr. Holloway, requesting an interview regarding river flooding.

Connor's stomach growled. He decided it was time for lunch. It was a sunny, spring day, a welcome relief from all the winter rain. Perfect time for a downtown stroll and lunch at his favorite eatery, Smooth Buns, a bakery and restaurant that drew rave reviews for its scrambled omelets.

The place, located on River Street on the ground level of a former brick warehouse, was crowded with diners.

Connor found a place at a table near the kitchen entrance. He ordered a scrambled Denver omelet and a glass of unsweet tea.

His mind was centered on all things floodwall and he didn't see two men approaching him from the kitchen. Oliver Essner and Truman Todt walked up to the table and sat down.

"Hey, guys. You sure are busy today," Connor remarked.

"Definitely. We like it that way," responded Oliver, who along with his husband, Truman, owned the eatery.

Oliver and Truman dressed far differently. Oliver wore old comfortable sweatshirts, jeans and tennis shoes. Truman favored designer jeans, long sleeved shirts and boots. Oliver was white; Truman, black. Connor and their other friends called them, "Salt and Pepper."

"You've been spending a lot of time writing about the damn floodwall," Truman said to Connor.

"That's true. This whole story is a perplexing puzzle."

"Any idea who defaced the wall?" Oliver asked.

"No. Not a clue. I did talk to Professor Carter. He shared with me some of the history of the floodwall. Clearly, the wall was designed to protect the downtown, not the south-side black community."

"Welcome to the 1950s and 1960s racism," remarked Truman. "I wasn't born until 1980. But I grew up on the south side in what was called Shantytown. We had paved roads by then, but our homes still flooded. The 1993 flood was the worst. After that, there was no going back. The federal flood buyout happened, and we found housing elsewhere in town."

"So, do you resent the floodwall?"

"You mean as a black person?" he asked, a little peeved by the question.

"I resent the fact town leaders back then didn't protect the black community from flooding."

"My family and I moved away from the river when I was 13. Decisions on where to build the floodwall are ancient history as far as I am concerned. Besides, I am a downtown business owner now. I want my business protected from the flooding and the floodwall does that."

"I understand, but can you think of anyone who would want to damage the floodwall?" he queried, looking at both Truman and Oliver.

22

"No," they both said in unison. Oliver added, "The floodwall is a part of the landscape now. The downtown used to be largely vacant buildings in the mid-90s. Now, it is a vibrant place, with unique restaurants, antique and gift shops and loft apartments above them. Who would want to wreck all that?"

CHAPTER SIX

Billy Moss was busy behind the Alligator Alley bar. The place was packed. It was a Friday night, two days after graffiti was discovered on the floodwall. Everyone from bankers to college students were hugging the bar, seeking booze to drown the end of another work week.

He was dressed in his usual attire: jeans and a college sweatshirt. He wiped the sweat from his brow as he hurried to the end of the bar to return change to one of his regular customers to whom he had just served a Bud Light draft.

Just hours earlier, detective Adam Dade had visited the downtown restaurant and grilled him for more than an hour.

Adam had suspected Billy had painted the message on the wall.

"I didn't do it," Billy told Adam. "But when I was walking back to my apartment the other night, I saw a man carrying a paint can and paint brush. He was about a block away from me, walking westward, away from the floodwall."

"Could you tell who it was?"

"No. It was too dark. He wasn't under a streetlight. He was tall. Looked like he was dressed in black. I didn't see any color in his clothes."

"Was he black or white?"

"I think he was white."

"Did he see you?"

"He turned slightly toward me," Billy remembered, then paused. "I think he saw me."

"Anything familiar about him?"

"The way he walked, reminded me of someone, but I just don't know who. A lot of people eat and drink here. It could have been a restaurant customer. I know the regulars at the bar. I don't pay as close attention to the restaurant customers. I see them walk by the bar, but I don't really look at them. They are just in the background as far as I'm concerned."

"So, do you think the same person who had you distribute those Bible verses defaced the wall?"

"I have no clue. It all seems crazy to me."

"Me too," responded Adam. "Me too."

As Billy replayed the conversation in his mind, he wondered if he had convinced Adam he didn't paint the horrible message on the wall. If only he hadn't been so willing to distribute those damn Bible verses. He wished he had never received those notes.

Billy's attention returned to his customers at the bar. He had just finished serving a good-looking woman a glass of House chardonnay when Elroy James barged in.

The mayor was his uncle. But Billy seldom interacted with Elroy. The two men had completely different personalities. Elroy liked to be the center of attention and could be arrogant at times. Billy preferred anonymity. He was soft spoken and liked to spend his leisure time hiking the trails at state parks in the region.

"What have you done?" Elroy yelled at Billy, thrusting his red face across the bar counter.

"What do you mean, Uncle?"

"The police told me that you distributed those threatening Bible verses. And now someone painted this graffiti threat on the floodwall."

"I didn't deface the floodwall. In fact, I think I may have seen the person who did."

"Who?"

"I couldn't tell. It was dark."

"How convenient," Elroy replied sarcastically. "You expect me to believe that?"

"Yes, I do."

"Well then you are a bigger fool than I thought. I'm warning you Billy, don't cross me. This is my town. If you're threatening this town, you are attacking me. And I won't stand for it."

Angered by Elroy's remarks, Billy lashed out. "What are you going to do, kill me?"

"Maybe," replied Elroy before turning and marching out of the restaurant as onlookers stared wide-eyed at the confrontation.

From the corner of the bar, Connor watched the dustup. He knew the mayor had a temper. He had been yelled at a few times himself. But as a reporter, nothing surprised him when it came to politicians and their dealings with the media.

But this surprised him. Elroy verbally whipping up on his own nephew.

"That was some conversation," Connor observed when Billy served him another draft beer.

"Yeah. Pretty intense. I've never seen my uncle so angry. I thought he was going to physically attack me. He was so mad."

"This flood stuff is eating away at him. The floodwall message seems like a personal affront to him. I am sure he'll calm down soon."

"Hope so," said Billy. "You know I didn't have anything to do with defacing the floodwall."

"I heard you proclaimed your innocence to Adam."

"I don't think he believed me."

"Adam is always skeptical. It's what makes him a good police detective."

"But you believe me, don't you?"

Connor stared at Billy. "Yes, I believe you. I just wish you could identify the man you saw with the paint can. Because in the eyes of the police right now, you're the only suspect they've got. And there is a lot of public pressure on the police to make an arrest, even if it means arresting an innocent man."

"Oh, jeez. This is a huge mess."

"Watch your back, Billy. Watch your back," advised Connor as he placed a $5 tip on the counter. Billy nodded and watched as Connor stepped down from the bar stool and headed out the door.

At a table in the back of the restaurant, the man with long graying hair smiled slightly. He had watched the confrontation. Everyone had heard the mayor yelling and threatening Billy. He hadn't expected that.

Dumb luck was on his side. It would make it easier to get rid of Billy now, he thought.

The man finished his spicy shrimp etouffee, washing it down with a cold mug of Schlafly Pale Ale.

He paid his bill, leaving a 20% tip for the college-aged waitress who thanked him with a broad smile before turning and walking to the kitchen.

The man watched her. "Nice ass," he said to himself. He would have liked to ask her out even though she was young enough to be his daughter. But he didn't have time for such an indulgence. He had work to do.

The river was still rising. Heavy rains over the past week in the Upper Midwest were sending a wall of water down river, putting more pressure on Elmwood's flood wall. The end was near and it excited him.

CHAPTER SEVEN

The professor was in. Tanner Holloway was seated at his desk in his corner office in the Elmwood College Science Center when Connor arrived.

Tanner had agreed to meet with Connor, who had explained to the environmental science professor that he wanted to interview him about the growing flood problem up and down the river.

"Come in. Come in," Tanner said, taking off his reading glasses, running his hand through his hair and putting aside the scientific journal he had been reading.

Connor estimated the professor was in his mid-40s, maybe older. He wore a forest green "Save the Planet" sweatshirt with an image of a gecko wrapped around the "P." A Cardinal baseball signed by Stan the Man Musial was displayed under a glass case on his desk.

"Thanks for seeing me," Connor said as he took a seat in a chair in front of the desk. "I see you are a Cardinal fan."

"Always have been. My dad and grandfather used to take me to games," Tanner replied before abruptly asking, "How can I help you?"

"I just wanted to talk to you about floodwalls."

"You mean like the one we have here?

"Yes."

"Does this have anything to do with that message on the floodwall I read about in the paper?"

"Well, yes. I just want to better understand why someone might hate floodwalls. I found an opinion piece you wrote a few years ago in the campus newspaper criticizing the Army Corps of Engineers and the policy of building even more levees and floodwalls."

"I assume you read it," Tanner began. "Not much has changed since then. Local, state and federal governments are only too eager to embrace floodwalls to allow for more commercial development in floodplains. It's a real shame."

28

"But don't floodwalls provide valuable protection against river flooding?"

"Not really. Actually, they make matters worse. We have walled off the rivers. Take the Mississippi, for example. We have constricted it, causing river levels to rise, risking catastrophic flooding. And for those areas with weaker levees or no levees at all, they are in danger of being wiped out by the force of the bottlenecked water being pushed downstream."

"So, what is the answer?"

"Tear down the levees and the floodwalls and let the rivers flow naturally over their banks and onto the floodplains like Mother Nature intended. The flooding would be more widespread, but less severe."

"But if you did that, Elmwood's downtown would be flooded."

"Well, you probably would have to tear down the buildings on River Street and turn it into a large pedestrian plaza. But it would be better for the environment. Of course, I don't think that would really happen. There's too much money tied up in commercial enterprises in our downtown to ever believe that would become a reality. Still, Mark Twain was right."

"In what way?" asked Connor.

"He once said, 'The Mississippi River will always have its own way; no engineering skill can persuade it to do otherwise.' Think about it, Connor. The Mississippi carries the mud of some 30 states and two Canadian provinces 2,000 miles south to the Gulf and deposits 500 million tons of it in the delta every year. And yet the Corps of Engineers is foolish enough to believe it can rein in the river."

"But would anyone really want to destroy Elmwood's floodwall?"

Tanner contemplated the question. His dark eyes stared at the office wall, covered in posters displaying photos of massive flooding on the Mississippi and Missouri rivers from previous floods. One showed a farmhouse, assaulted by floodwaters up to its roof. In another, people with their precious belongings in pillowcases boated through a flood ravaged street.

"Talk to the folks across the river in East Elmwood. Earthen levees protect the village, but they are not as high as the concrete floodwall, nor as strong. The floodwall pushes back on the river, forcing the high water to gouge away at the earthen levees. Those folks have every reason to hate the floodwall."

"Enough to destroy it?"

"You never know how people will act when their very existence is threatened," Tanner replied.

"True. It's worth checking out."

Tanner eyed the clock on the wall. "I have a class to teach in 10 minutes. But if you have any other questions don't hesitate to call me. Good luck with your story."

"Thanks," said Connor, putting away his reporter's notebook and heading for the door.

After Connor left, Tanner googled the local flood stage on his phone. The National Weather Service forecast called for the river to reach 47 feet soon, only five feet below the top of the wall and certain catastrophe. He could feel a disaster brewing in this river city and wondered if anything could stop it.

CHAPTER EIGHT

Connor drove south on River Street, headed for the four-lane cable stay bridge that towered over the swollen Mississippi River.

The river was so high now that from a distance barges looked like they were riding along the floodwall.

Connor turned onto the bridge and traveled across it. East Elmwood was little more than a cluster of run-down trailers, one small subdivision and the only real business in town – the strip club.

Perched along the state highway, Club Mardi Gras was a one-story, green and gold building. An elevated sign outside displayed the name in neon along with an image of a naked woman pole dancing.

The club owner, an Asian woman named Marissa Hue, also owned the other two businesses in town: a pizza parlor and a convenience store.

The club parking lot was empty now. It was only midday. The crowd wouldn't show until around midnight. Having partied in bars on the Missouri side, they would then cross the bridge to enjoy the club. Men, many of them college students, would ogle the women and tuck dollar bills in the dancers' G-strings or pay for private lap dances.

Sometimes the club would feature Penthouse models or other celebrity dancers who made a good living taking off their clothes. But mostly the dancers were in their late teens or early 20s, some of them college students. Others were single moms, some of them victims of domestic violence, just looking for a way out of poverty. On a good night, a dancer could make a thousand dollars, a better wage than anywhere else in the worn-out village.

Connor pulled into the convenience store parking lot, across the street from the club. The lot was being used as a staging area for Illinois National Guard troops and volunteers who were piling sandbags atop an earthen levee to help hold back the river.

He saw East Elmwood's mayor, 66-year old Harvey Winston,

directing volunteers in the flood fight.

"Harvey, how is your town holding up?" asked Connor.

"It's touch and go right now," said Harvey, who had served as mayor for more than a decade. His jeans and shirt were stained with sand and mud. Even though the temperature was still in the mid-60s with a northerly breeze, Harvey was sweating through his shirt. He was wearing a pair of dark leather cowboy boots, the color blending with the caked-on mud. A cigarette dangled from his mouth.

"I've never seen the river this high. And it's not just the river, it's the seep water we have to contend with," he said, pointing toward flooded farm fields bordering the village. There was so much water it looked like a huge lake. White egrets and other waterfowl crowded into the fields.

"You got enough volunteers?"

"For now. The Illinois National Guard sent over some troops. Plus, we have help from the county's highway department which has been hauling in sandbags."

"I was wondering if the floodwall across the river makes things worse for East Elmwood?"

"A lot of people here would say so. It's a fuckin' nightmare for us Illinois folk.," he said, stopping to take a drag of his Camel cigarette, the smoke hanging in the air. "Before the floodwall was built, the river flooded Elmwood's downtown nearly every spring, but it resulted in less flooding over here. But since the erection of the wall, flooding over here has just gotten worse each and every year, it seems."

"Would anyone be mad enough to tear down the wall?"

"You mean blow it up like the Missouri Department of Transportation did with the old Mississippi River bridge some years ago after the new span was completed?'

"Yeah. Something like that."

"That would be crazy. Nobody in their right mind would attempt it."

"What about somebody not in their right mind? Can you think of anyone who would be crazy enough to do that?"

"No one comes to mind. Why? You think someone intends to damage the wall?"

"I don't know. But someone wrote a threatening message on the floodwall and I am trying to figure out if the threat should be taken seriously."

Out of the corner of his eye, Connor spied Hue approaching. He had interviewed her only a month ago after one of her dancers had been wounded in a shooting on the parking lot by two customers who fled in a dark-colored SUV. So far, no one had been arrested.

"Hey, Mr. Tate. How are you doing?"

"Fine, Marissa. What's going on?"

"I am helping with the flood fight. The club has a full kitchen. I had my staff make some sandwiches for the volunteers. I appreciate their efforts to try to keep the town and my club above water."

"Did you hear about the message left on the floodwall?"

"I read about it in the paper. Do you take the threat seriously?"

"I don't know how to take it. I know city officials worry that someone intends to do serious harm."

"Blow a hole in the wall? That seems highly unlikely," she observed.

"Still, it's what has community leaders losing sleep at night."

"What keeps me awake is something else. Will our earthen levee hold? If the river tops the levee our village will drown, and that's scary."

The mayor nodded in agreement. "We have pumps running around the clock, but it won't be enough if the river rises much more. We may have to evacuate the town."

"I hope not," said Connor. "If the river continues to rise, the city of Elmwood will be flooded too. We'll all be in the same boat."

"Yeah," said Harvey. "We'll be paddling for our lives."

CHAPTER NINE

The crowd was rowdy the last Saturday night of March. Too little sunshine and a stiff, spring breeze made everyone restless. Time to party.

There was an hour long wait for tables. Billy Moss poured drinks at the bar, mostly Bud Lights and Pale Ales. The talk of the bar turned to the St. Louis Cardinals and the start of the baseball season. Elmwood was Cardinal country. Those who wore blue Cubs hats were automatically suspect.

Although he was busy, Billy couldn't keep his mind off his recollections of a man with a paint can who walked with long strides and back straight as an arrow. He'd seen him somewhere recently. He was sure of it.

Even with two people working the bar, Billy was constantly on the move, filling drink orders all night long. By the time the bar closed at 1:30 a.m., he was exhausted. He and the other employees began cleaning up. One by one, his co-workers left. Billy was usually the last to leave. He liked it that way. It gave him time to unwind. Time to be alone with his own thoughts, images swirling of the mystery man with the paint can and the troubling message on the floodwall.

He couldn't shake the thought that he had seen the man somewhere. Could he have seen the man dining in Alligator Alley? He increasingly thought so.

He had been too busy to take even a small break earlier, to go smoke. At 2:15 a.m., 45 minutes after the place closed, Billy decided to smoke a cigarette. He walked through the now empty restaurant, his footsteps echoing across the hardwood floor, worn smooth by its more than a century of use as a riverfront warehouse now turned eatery. The place was deadly silent. Everyone else had finished their shift and gone home.

He moved through the cleaned-up kitchen, dishes neatly stacked away, and opened the back door. Billy stepped outside and eyed the darkness. A streetlight glowed near the other end of the building. He sat down on the concrete steps, illuminated by a low-watt light fixture attached to the building's brick wall. Billy lit a Marlboro and inhaled the addicting nicotine, exhaling a rising wisp of smoke.

From the corner of his eye, he saw a man approaching from a nearby alley. The man walked unsteadily. Probably a drunk. Billy was used to seeing drunks stumble around behind the restaurant after closing time.

But the closer the man came, the steadier he seemed, taking long strides. Strange, Billy thought.

The man was dressed all in black. Even his ball cap was black. He cast his eyes downward. He kept his gloved hands in his jacket pockets.

He was about five feet away when he looked up. He smiled at Billy, who nodded even as the thought hit the tired bartender: this was the guy with the paint can, no doubt the floodwall vandal.

The man stared straight at Billy as he thumbed the safety off and pulled a semi-automatic pistol from his jacket in one quick motion. He fired two shots into Billy's head. Billy slumped over, blood dripping down his face, pooling on the steps. It happened so fast that Billy never moved before being fatally shot.

The man looked around. The discharges had been loud to his ears. But he saw no witnesses. No one was running to the scene. The man concluded anyone who heard the shots might have thought it was a car backfiring. Or maybe anyone in earshot was too drunk to notice.

From his pants pocket, he removed a short strip of paper on which he had typed one word: "DROWNED." Holding the paper in his gloved right hand, he bent down and placed the paper atop Billy's lifeless forehead, the paper sticking to the bloody edge around the .45 caliber bullet holes.

The man retreated into the dark alley, headed for his vehicle parked three blocks away behind a vacant, soon-to-be-razed house. Once in his vehicle, he removed the pistol and stuck it in the glovebox. He would hide it when he got home. He knew he probably should throw it in the river and let the floodwaters take it downstream, to be lost forever. But he couldn't bring himself to do that. The pistol was ancient. He loved holding the weapon and shooting it. It made him feel invincible even as a teenager when he longed for a caring dad, something his father was not.

His father had been a used-car salesman in Southern Illinois, a violent drunk who regularly beat up his mom. His dad ended up going to prison for fatally strangling his mother. He died there from cirrhosis of the liver five years ago. He was a fucking, horrible person. It was about time he died.

Family members refused to bury him. They left it up to the Illinois Department of Corrections, which had him cremated and his ashes buried in an unmarked grave in Springfield, the state capital.

The pistol was an heirloom. The man wouldn't part with it. It was too precious. Besides, he reasoned, no one would suspect him of killing that bartender.

He had done his homework. He had watched Billy for weeks, learning his routine. He knew Billy always left last. Always liked to smoke before heading home from work. Terrible habit, smoking. It can kill you. Just ask Billy.

Billy wasn't an innocent bystander, reasoned the pistol-packing man. His great-grandfather was the damn mayor who championed the building of the floodwall. The whole family had blood on its hands, maybe not literally. But the floodwall was a killer and Billy's grandfather enabled that wall to be built. Killing him was justice, rough justice maybe, but it was still justice, the man concluded. And it made him smile.

CHAPTER TEN

An army of uniformed officers, detectives and criminal investigators congregated around the lifeless body of Billy Moss.

It was 7 a.m. on a Sunday. Most downtown businesses were closed for the day. Connor had planned to take a hike on his off day as the forecast called for sunshine and temperatures in the high 60s. Perfect for a walk on one of his favorite trails, a 3-mile route across a hilly, wooded area near the Missouri Conservation Department's regional nature center.

But instead he was camped out at the crime scene. He saw Adam, dressed in a suit and tie. There was a visible bulge on his hip where a Glock pistol was lodged in a holster.

Connor waved Adam over. "Anything you can tell me?"

"About the shooting?"

"No, about the weather," Connor sarcastically replied.

"Yeah. Well we don't know much yet." Adam looked around to make sure the chief was not in earshot. "You didn't hear it from me, but the victim was Billy Moss. He was shot twice in the head. It looks like he died instantly. But officially you will have to get that from the chief. He plans to hold a news conference soon. The coroner is on the scene. We should be moving the body soon."

"I wonder if Billy's death has anything to do with the floodwall matter?" Connor asked.

"Wouldn't surprise me. Billy told me he saw a man carrying a paint can on a downtown street near the floodwall around 3 one morning. Maybe that man was afraid Billy might identify him."

"Kill someone over graffiti?"

"But what if it's more than that," wondered Adam. "What if that man wants to blow up the floodwall?"

"As high as the river now is, a breach of the floodwall could devastate the downtown."

"Exactly. Maybe all the more reason why someone would be willing to kill Billy," said Adam.

Connor waited around, observing the investigation. Police roped off the area with yellow crime-scene tape. Detectives and uniformed officers began looking for possible witnesses. Family members of the victim stood nearby, shocked looks on their faces. How could this have happened?

The mayor showed up, driving up the alley in his white Cadillac. The chief saw him as soon as he left the vehicle.

Even from a distance, Connor could tell Elroy was demanding answers. Chief Bonney didn't have any answers, not yet.

Forty-five minutes later, the coroner having removed the body for an autopsy, the chief held a news conference behind the restaurant, near the crime scene. A crowd of reporters and news photographers and videographers showed up. Connor stood near the front, a digital recorder in his hand.

"As you all probably know," the chief began, "there was a shooting. Billy Moss, a bartender at Alligator Alley was killed. He was shot twice in the head, appears to be from a semiautomatic pistol. The coroner believes Billy died instantly."

"When did the shooting happen?" asked a short, 20-something, purple sports coat-clad reporter for a local TV station.

"The coroner estimates the shooting happened early this morning, probably shortly after the restaurant closed. The place closed at 1:30 a.m. That's all I can say right now, except to encourage anyone who may have seen something suspicious down here last night to call the police department."

With that, the chief retreated toward his officers, ignoring shouted questions.

Connor watched Tyler shooting with a zoom lens as police continued to work the scene. Connor didn't stay much longer. There was a story to write. He hurried back to the newsroom.

Lansmon met him at his desk. "What's the story?"

"Murder. Billy Moss, Alligator Alley's bartender who was the mayor's nephew, was shot to death behind the restaurant. Police recently questioned him about the threatening message on the floodwall. Don't think he wrote the message. But police don't know if the murder is related to the message somehow or to those earlier Bible verses about flooding."

"Well, make sure you get all that in the story. People are antsy enough about all the flooding and the message on the floodwall. This murder will only make people more upset."

"Yeah. And there's something else."

"What?"

"I was at the restaurant recently. I saw the mayor get into an argument with Billy. I heard Elroy threaten Billy. A lot of people did."

"That is interesting. Check it out. Call the mayor. Ask him why he threatened Billy. I can't imagine the mayor as a killer. But we need to track down as much information as we can."

Connor nodded and returned to his desk, piled high with printed notes and files for a wide range of stories he was working on, including one on cost overruns associated with a major street project. But those stories would have to wait.

He picked up the phone and called the mayor. Elroy answered on the fourth ring.

"What do you want?" said the mayor, who had caller ID.

"I am sorry for your loss, but I have some questions about your nephew. What was he like as a person?"

"He was a great guy. Loved life. Can't imagine why anyone would kill him."

"But I was at the restaurant the other day when you threatened him. Lots of people heard you threaten to kill him."

"I didn't mean it. You can't think I would do that," pleaded Elroy. "I was just mad. I knew from the police that Billy had distributed those Bible verses about flooding. I was concerned that he may have painted the threatening message on the wall. Billy didn't always think before he acted. I was afraid he had done something stupid. I wanted him to quit messing around with all this talk of drowning."

"I get it, but I am sure police will be asking you about it."

"Well, let them," Elroy said angrily. "I have nothing to hide." He slammed down the phone.

CHAPTER ELEVEN

The call came the next day as Elroy was eating a bowl of cereal and drinking a cup of hazelnut coffee at his kitchen table.

It was Blair. "Can you come down to the station, Elroy? We have a few questions to ask you in connection with your nephew's death."

"I figured you would be calling, Blair. Hope you are not trying to pin the murder on me. I didn't do it."

"I'm not saying you did. We just want to talk to you."

"I'll be there within the hour. Hopefully, this won't take too long. I need to get down to the funeral home. The family wants to make arrangements for the funeral service."

"I understand. It shouldn't take long. Just ask for me when you get here."

Elroy finished breakfast and got dressed. He picked out a blue Oxford shirt and a striped, blue tie to go with his navy-colored suit and his polished, black dress shoes.

He was mayor and he wanted his attire to demonstrate he was in charge, not the police chief. Blair was not going to pull rank on him. He would make that clear.

Arriving at the station Elroy greeted a few of the longtime officers as he was escorted into a conference room.

"Thanks for coming," Blair said. "You know detective Adam Dade. He is sitting in on this interview."

Elroy sat across from Blair and the detective. He noticed Adam had turned on a digital recorder.

"Am I under suspicion?" Elroy asked.

"In the police department, we suspect everyone until we can rule them out," responded Blair, who was dressed in his police uniform rather than his usual suit.

"We have interviewed some witnesses to a recent dispute you had with Billy. What happened?

Elroy stared harshly at the chief. He hated having to recount the argument.

40

"I found out that my nephew had distributed those Bible verses, putting the fear of God in people about the flood. It was a stupid thing for him to do and I told him so. Billy was a nice young man, but he didn't always use his brain."

"I understand you thought Billy might have been responsible for the threatening message on the floodwall." Adam asked.

"Yes, the thought had occurred to me. I made that clear to Billy."

"You threatened to kill Billy," the chief said.

"Now, Blair, you know I wouldn't kill anyone."

"Still, a lot of people heard you threaten him."

"I know. I was just angry about Billy distributing those Bible verses. I figured he knew who put him up to it. I wanted him to tell me. People are worried enough about the rising floodwaters. There are rumors out there that the wall won't hold. Everyone it seems is predicting a disaster. You need to find out what's going on here. Find the person who put that awful message on the wall and arrest his ass."

"I understand your concern," said Blair, "but right now the focus is on who killed Billy and why."

"Well, I didn't do it."

"So, you've said. Can you think of anyone who might want Billy dead?"

"No. Most people liked Billy. He would talk to anyone and everyone with whom he crossed paths."

"Didn't he get in an argument with one of the downtown business owners a few years ago?"

"Yeah. Billy was upset when Ronnie Diebold refused to lease an empty storefront to Billy, who wanted to open his own bar. Ronnie wouldn't rent to him because he felt Billy was too young to go into business for himself. He doubted Billy could make a go of it."

"What did Billy do?" asked Adam, inserting himself back into the conversation.

"He told everyone that Ronnie was a bad landlord, who charged tenants exorbitant leases and could care less about the merchants that called downtown home."

"Did Ronnie threaten Billy?" asked Adam.

"I heard he said he would shut him up if he kept making such

41

allegations, but that's just hearsay. I personally never heard him say such a thing. Anyway, all that talk occurred years ago."

"We'll follow up on it, but I don't see Ronnie as a likely suspect," Blair said. "For one thing, I doubt he even owns a gun. I've seen his Facebook page. It's full of rants against the NRA."

"Where were you around the time of the murder?"

"I was at home."

"Your wife can confirm that?"

Elroy bit his lip. "No, I was alone. My wife was in St. Louis visiting her sister."

"How convenient. So, we only have your word that you were not downtown confronting Billy and shooting him."

"My word should be good enough," Elroy snarled.

"Do you own a gun?" Blair asked.

"You know I do. I own a Winchester Model 94 rifle. I use it when I go deer hunting every fall."

"Own any other guns?"

"No. I don't own a handgun. Never even shot one. Are we done? I have to get to the funeral home."

"Yes, for now. If we have any more questions, we'll call you."

"I am sure you will," replied Elroy, clearly frustrated by all the questions.

Elroy walked quickly through the station and out the front door where he was greeted by a throng of reporters yelling questions at him.

"Did you kill the bartender?" asked one young blonde TV reporter, dressed in a tight blue pants suit.

"I didn't kill my nephew. Anyone who suggests that is the case is a liar," he angrily responded, pushing reporters out of his way as he walked to his Cadillac.

"So why did the police interview you?" a longtime police reporter for a local TV station asked.

"Just routine. They asked me to give them a statement and I did."

"But you threatened your nephew, Alligator Alley customers say," the reporter said.

"I spoke in anger, but I didn't kill him," Elroy shouted as TV crews and news photographers captured images of him getting into his car.

"Damn that Blair," Elroy said as he drove away. He knew Blair had tipped off the news media that he was being interviewed at the police station.

When Elroy's wife had been arrested for shoplifting, Blair had refused to drop the case. In response, Elroy had orchestrated a cut in funding for the police department, forcing the chief to reduce staff.

Elroy slammed his fist on the dashboard as he headed to the funeral home. Elmwood needed a new police chief, someone competent, who would actually solve the case and arrest Billy's murderer. Blair wasn't the only one who could play to the press, Elroy told himself.

Elroy didn't watch the local TV news that night. He knew his visit to the police station would lead the news. It also would be on the front page of the paper the next morning.

But one man paid very close attention to the news, the public attention drawn to the mayor as a possible murder suspect. His plot was evolving.

CHAPTER TWELVE

Connor sat at his desk, writing the story on the mayor's police station interview. He had been part of the crowd of reporters, had seen the mayor's angry reaction.

Connor knew the mayor and chief didn't get along. The chief wanted the mayor to have to appear at the police station, wanted to publicly shame him. Why else did Bare Bones alert the media to Elroy's appearance at the police station.

He finished the story and marked it ready to edit online. He was thinking of taking an early lunch when the phone rang. Connor looked at the caller ID. He didn't recognize the number. He thought of just letting the call go to voice mail, but at the last minute decided to answer it.

"This is Connor Tate. Can I help you?"

"I just want to know why you all have never reported anything about the stolen dynamite?"

"What stolen dynamite?"

"The dynamite stolen from the quarry," the raspy male voice responded.

"The local quarry on the city's south side?"

"Yeah. Southeast Missouri Bootheel Quarry."

"You say dynamite was stolen. When was this?"

"About six months ago. A whole container of dynamite was taken, about 50 pounds of it."

"How do you know about it?"

"I am a heavy equipment operator at the place. I won't give you my name. I don't want to get in trouble with the company."

"Was it reported to police?"

"I think the company reported it, but asked police to keep it out of the police report."

"Police never disclosed the incident to the paper. Do you know any particulars about how the theft occurred?"

"No, but I know the dynamite was taken from a secure storage building."

44

"What made you decide to call now?"

"Well, with the death of that bartender and the floodwall threat, I just got to thinking – maybe someone stole the dynamite to blow up the floodwall. I thought maybe you could check into it."

"I'll do that," Connor replied just before the caller hung up. "Damn," he said aloud as he contemplated what he had just heard.

"What's wrong?" asked Rachel seated at her desk where she was putting together a story on a school bond issue.

"I've just found out that someone stole a whole bunch of dynamite from the quarry about six months ago and the caller wondered if the explosives might be used to blow up the floodwall."

"God, that's an awful thought," she said.

Connor briefly forgot about the dynamite as he glanced her way, observing the way her body moved beneath a lacy black blouse and blue jeans. Maybe I should ask her out, he thought before quickly turning his attention back to the dynamite.

"You think there could be any truth to someone wanting to blow up the wall?" asked Rachel.

"Maybe. It could explain the Bible verses and the threatening messages. I need to talk to the police and see what they know."

Connor rose and walked swiftly across the newsroom and out the door. He wanted to talk to Adam in private.

From his Ford Escape, he called Adam's cell phone. The two friends agreed to meet at Smooth Buns.

Connor arrived first at the downtown bakery and restaurant. It was lunchtime and the place was packed. He chose a small table in a corner of the place.

Adam arrived 10 minutes later. He strode into the restaurant, his Glock holstered on his hip under his brown sports coat and joined Connor at the table. Both ordered spinach quiches and raspberry tea.

"What's so urgent that you couldn't tell me over the phone?" Adam asked.

"Did you know that dynamite is missing from the quarry?"

"I heard we received a report to that effect about six months ago."

"You didn't see the report?"

"Quarry officials wanted to keep it hush-hush. They made a report for insurance reasons, but they didn't want us to put it down on the police report that we give to the news media. They were afraid if it got out in the public, it might encourage more thefts from the quarry, which, as you know, is in a more isolated area. How did you hear about it?

"An anonymous caller said he worked at the quarry. He worried that the dynamite could be used to blow up the floodwall."

"I hadn't thought of that," replied Adam, his mind racing over the possibility.

"Did you ever find the dynamite?" asked Connor.

"No. Nor the other stuff."

"What other stuff?"

"The detonating cord that is used to simultaneously discharge a number of explosives."

"So how did the thief or thieves get access to the dynamite?"

"They broke into a storage building. Climbed into a locked, concrete room through a ventilation shaft."

"Do you think the caller could be right, that someone wants to damage the floodwall?" Connor asked as the waitress brought their meals to the table.

"It's possible, but I wouldn't go off the deep end. The graffiti and the Bible verses don't point me in the direction of some deranged bomber. And what I've told you Connor, you can't use."

"I don't intend to burn my favorite source. I just wanted some background. I think it is possible someone wants to flood the downtown."

"And you think that motive could be connected to Billy's murder?"

"Yes, I do. But so far I've been unable to connect all the dots."

"Be careful, Connor. I know you like investigative reporting. But if you are right, there is a murderer out there who might kill again to protect his destructive plan."

"Don't worry. I won't try to be a hero. I just want to expose anyone who would seek to engage in such destruction." Adam nodded in agreement even though he worried Connor would take risks in search of the truth. Finding it, he knew, wouldn't be easy.

CHAPTER THIRTEEN

The sandbags didn't stop the relentless water. Neither did the tons of dirt and rock piled atop the old earthen levee protecting East Elmwood from the onslaught. Even the huge portable pumps, running nonstop to suck up the water and empty it downstream, weren't enough.

In early April, East Elmwood residents woke up to find their small town awash in floodwater. The raging river had breached the levee sometime after midnight, sending a wall of water washing over the town and nearby farm fields. The whole area looked like one big lake. And still the water poured in.

Strip-club owner Marissa Hue watched the horrifying scene from the front entrance of Club Mardi Gras, along with Mayor Harvey Winston.

The club sat on a slightly elevated tract of land, which so far was not flooded. Its parking lot, however, sat slightly lower and was filling up with water. The highway through town looked like a roaring river. The pavement was nowhere to be seen, covered with muddy water.

"I've never seen anything like it in all my years," the mayor said, having walked through floodwaters in hip waders from his house two blocks south of the club."

"Neither have I, Harvey. We've got a disaster on our hands," Marissa observed.

"The water is probably at least two feet deep on some sections of the road. The state police are setting up roadblocks to keep motorists away from the flooding. The highway department plans to bring in more rock and dirt to try to shore up the levee, but there's no guarantee they can make much headway right now," sighed Harvey.

It was 9 a.m. when Connor and Tyler headed over the bridge toward the disaster. State police cars had blocked eastbound traffic at the Illinois end of the bridge.

Connor and Tyler climbed out of Connor's SUV. Showing their

press badges to the state trooper, they walked about 50 more feet, near where the murky floodwaters covered the highway.

Tyler began clicking away, capturing the watery destruction, on his digital camera.

A white pickup truck sat stalled on the shoulder of the highway; its engine flooded out. The driver had waded through the high water to dry pavement on the bridge.

Some residents, who arose early, had managed to move their vehicles onto the safety of the bridge. Now they were ferrying clothes and personal items from their homes in flat-bottomed boats or carrying suitcases over their heads as they walked through the water.

Connor saw Marissa and Harvey aiding residents trying to reach higher ground. Others were lending a hand too, including professor Tanner Holloway.

Tanner, outfitted in rubber waders, was pulling a rowboat, filled with a distraught mother and her two young children, to the safety of the bridge.

Tanner saw Connor and waved to him. As soon as he beached the boat on dry ground, he walked over to Connor.

"I didn't expect to see you out here?" Connor said.

"I grew up over here. I know these folks. I wanted to help. I only have two classes to teach today and they're evening classes. When I heard on the news about the flooding, I decided to come right over."

"That's nice of you."

"We all need to help our neighbors."

"You told me in your office that the Missouri floodwall put more pressure on the East Elmwood levee, putting residents here at greater risk of flooding."

"Yes, and as you can see, I was proven right."

"So, if someone had blown up the Elmwood floodwall, the flooding situation in East Elmwood would have been alleviated?"

"Yes. Basic hydrology would tell you that's the case. The river dropped a foot on the Elmwood gauge overnight after the East Elmwood levee broke."

"By your thinking then, residents on this side of the river would benefit from blowing up the Elmwood floodwall."

"I would say so."

"So, would you favor the flooding of Elmwood's downtown?"

"Hypothetically, yes. But you don't see me tearing down the wall. I'm simply arguing policy, not vandalism. Got a go. I need to wade through the water again. There are other residents here I need to help," said Tanner.

"Thanks for the chat," Connor said, wondering to himself who else might want to tear down the wall. Did someone in East Elmwood want to destroy the aging wall? Was that person also a murderer? All these questions and still no answers.

Connor spied Tyler hitching a ride in another boat manned by volunteers who were seeking to rescue residents trapped in their homes.

Connor turned his attention to the flood victims, interviewing adults and children alike for more than 30 minutes.

He had finished doing the interviews when he was approached by Marissa and Harvey, who had made countless trips through the muddy water.

"It's bad," Harvey said, not bothering with small talk.

"I see that. Do you expect any more help?"

"Illinois National Guard is mobilizing more troops as well as trucks to haul in dirt and rock and bulldozers to make temporary repairs to the levee in hopes of closing the breach," he said.

"Marissa, it looks like your club is still high and dry," Connor said eyeing her.

"Yes. But I don't know for how long. At any rate, I'll still have to shut down the club until the water goes down. It will definitely cost me money."

"And the town money, too," chimed in Harvey. "Marissa's club is the big money maker in town. East Elmwood depends on the sales taxes generated by her establishment to pay for basic city services."

"Who knew that lap dances could be so lucrative," Connor quipped.

Marissa grinned broadly. "I do my part for the community," she said, "and, of course, the gentlemen who want our services."

"You guys know Tanner?" Connor asked.

"Oh, yes, he's originally from here. It's nice of him to help out," Harvey said.

"Tanner blames the Elmwood floodwall for making things

worse for you all. Do you share that thought?"

"Of course," Marissa said. "We all know the elephant in the room, so to speak, is that damn floodwall. It constricts the river, forcing the water higher. Our smaller levee can't hold up."

Marissa saw Connor's serious look. "Don't jump to conclusions, Connor. I'm not suggesting I would blow up the wall."

"I didn't say that."

"But you thought that might be a possibility," she replied.

"Same for me," Harvey said. "I am not a bomber. But I'll be honest, I wouldn't shed a tear if some of the floodwater fell on the Missouri side."

"There appear to be lots of folks who have the same opinion," said Connor before heading back to the newsroom. He had a story to write, one that probably no one on the Missouri side would want to hear.

CHAPTER FOURTEEN

Connor sat at his desk, typing up a story on the flood fight across the river, punctuated by the animosity of East Elmwood residents toward the massive floodwall on the Missouri shore.

Connor wrote a one-sentence lead: "As floodwaters devastate East Elmwood, Illinois, residents there look with loathing at the concrete floodwall across the river, the gray monster they believe is destroying their community."

"How's the flood fight?" asked Rachel, stopping by Connor's desk.

"It's dire in East Elmwood. But what is really surprising is how much residents blame their flood woes on our floodwall. And it's not just them. Tanner, that Elmwood College professor, shares their view."

"So, is the graffiti artist maybe an East Elmwood resident? And, is that someone who would try to damage the wall?"

"I don't know. What I do know is there's a lot of anger over there."

"Enough to murder?"

"Possibly, but so far there is no evidence Billy's murder is connected to the floodwall vandalism."

"No, but it could be," replied Rachel.

"Yes, it could be."

Connor's story ran at the top of the front page the next day. He had barely settled into his desk chair that morning when his office phone rang. Tanner was on the phone.

"I just wanted to congratulate you, Connor, on your story today. You disclosed what many people feel about that floodwall. Hopefully, it will enlighten your Missouri readers."

"I was just doing my job, conveying how people in East Elmwood feel about the wall."

"Well, you did a great job."

"Thanks. I'm sure we'll talk again about floodwalls and flooding."

"You can count on it," said Tanner, ending the conversation.

"Who was that?" asked Rachel, seated at the adjacent desk.

"That was Tanner."

"He and you seem to be chatting a lot these days," she said, her thick hair flowing onto her shoulders, framing her smiling eyes.

"Yeah. Well, he seems fixated on the floodwall."

"Enough to damage it?"

"I don't know, but it's hard to conceive of an Elmwood College professor as an environmentalist terrorist."

"True, but it's not like such a person is hanging out a shingle, advertising that fact."

"You've got a point," said Connor. "I'll keep it in mind."

***

Police Chief Blair Bonney was in his office reconciling budget figures for his department when Adam walked in.

"You've got to see this chief," he said, turning on the wall-mounted television. The local station was broadcasting a news conference with the mayor.

Elroy was standing in front of the floodwall. Reporters and news photographers and videographers gathered around.

Elroy was talking about Billy's murder.

"Billy's murder has shaken this community. It's time for our police chief and our police department to update Elmwood residents on the status of their murder investigation. We need answers, not excuses."

"Son of a bitch," observed Blair. "He's trying to throw me under the bus. What an ass."

"He's throwing the entire police department under the bus," Adam interrupted.

On TV, Elroy continued to question why the department had not made an arrest yet. "I am not demanding justice for Billy's family because Billy was my nephew. I am demanding justice because every resident of Elmwood should receive justice regardless of their station in life. Our city is in the midst of this community's biggest flood fight. This community is already on edge. Solving this murder would go a long way toward helping our citizens move forward. Yet, even now, the police are not keeping your mayor or other city leaders informed about the murder investigation. We need answers."

"Fuck him," Blair said, jumping up from his chair. "He wants to get in a public feud. I will give him one. Set up a news conference for this afternoon in front of the police station. I will give the public an update and show everyone what a jerk the mayor is."

"You better be careful," Adam warned. "You don't want to get fired."

"The mayor can't fire me, only the city manager."

"But the city council can fire the city manager."

"They could, but most of the council members view the mayor as a pompous ass. They'll take my side over his," the chief insisted.

By 2 p.m., the news media had gathered outside the police station, located near the city's fairgrounds, several miles from Elmwood's downtown.

"Thanks for coming," the chief began. "As you know, the mayor earlier today suggested that I and the police department in general had not kept him informed about the murder investigation. He is correct in that we have deliberately not reached out to him because witnesses reported seeing him threaten the victim, Billy Moss, shortly before the fatal shooting. As a result, it would have been improper for police to communicate with the mayor while the investigation continues. Rest assured, we are doing everything in our power to bring to justice the criminal who shot Billy."

Connor asked, "Chief, are you saying that the mayor remains a suspect?"

"I did not say that. What I said is that there is evidence he threatened Billy. As such, we are following up to see if there is reason to take an even closer look at the mayor. So far, we have no solid evidence which would indicate the mayor killed Billy. But we owe it to the citizens to check out every lead even if it might involve an elected official."

"Have you found the person who painted the threatening message on the floodwall?" another reporter asked.

"No, we have not."

"Is the vandalism connected to the murder?" Connor asked.

"We are looking into that possibility."

The news conference lasted only about 20 minutes. Seated back in his office a short time later, Blair grinned broadly. The news conference went well, he thought.

He called Adam into his office. "I think it's time we have another chat with Elroy, and we need to get a search warrant. We need to find that damn gun."

"Elroy said he doesn't own such a pistol," Adam said.

"That's so, but how do we know he isn't lying," the chief replied. "Maybe a search will give us the answer."

"You think a judge will sign off on a search warrant involving the mayor?"

"Yeah. I think I can get it."

"You could be getting the department into a political firestorm," Adam observed.

"I know, but we have to do something. I am not going to allow that clown of a mayor to cast doubt on the fine men and women in the police department. We are going to do our jobs and follow the evidence where it leads us. If the mayor's the killer, we're going to find out."

Blair found Judge Donald Fisher in his courthouse office eating a tuna sandwich for lunch. He had been on the bench for decades, having been reelected time and time again. At age 69, he was looking forward to finishing out the year and retiring. No more criminals to sentence. No more lawyers making tiresome arguments. No more exhausting trials. He could finally find time to relax in his cabin along Current River, away from the hustle and bustle of the law.

"Hey, Chief, what brings you to court?" the judge asked, looking up.

"Judge, I need you to sign a search warrant."

"Another drug case?"

"No. A murder case. Billy Moss's murder," said Blair, handing him the paperwork.

Judge Fisher read the information, which had been agreed to by the prosecutor. Finally, he looked up, a shocked expression on his face.

"You want me to approve a search warrant to search the house and office of the mayor for possible evidence? Are you crazy?"

"No. I really think we need to do this search, not play favorites. If anyone else had threatened Billy in front of witnesses, we would have already conducted such a search."

"But this isn't just another suspect. You are suggesting this city's mayor could be a murderer. That's daring on your part, I will give you that."

"It's also the right thing to do," Blair said.

"Maybe. Or maybe you're just pissed that the mayor unloaded on you and your department at his news conference. Are you sure you want to proceed with this? It's not too late to back off?"

"No, Judge. I want to proceed. Who knows, when it is all said and done, this might clear the mayor."

"Even so, you might be looking for another job when this is all over, Blair."

"True, but I am willing to take that chance."

Judge Fisher sighed, then signed the search warrant. "I hope you know what you are doing, Blair."

"Thanks, Judge. Wish me luck," the chief said, exiting the judge's office.

"You may be out of luck, Chief," Judge Fisher replied, shaking his head over what had just happened.

CHAPTER FIFTEEN

Maj. Gen. Ted Walsh of the Army Corps of Engineers Memphis District looked every bit the part of a military commander, his starched olive-green uniform and polished Army boots conveying a man who liked everything in its place.

He and his staff members visited Elmwood near the end of the first week of April to reassure city leaders and the public that the aging floodwall would hold in the wake of unprecedented high water.

The river initially had dropped when the Illinois levee broke, but now it was on the rise again. The roiling river now stood at 49 feet on the Elmwood gauge, three feet below the top of the wall, and climbing. Heavy rains up north were now sending more water rampaging downstream toward Southeast Missouri and Southern Illinois.

"We expect the Mississippi to crest by the end of April, although some forecasts suggest the flooding could continue into May. Still, we don't expect it to top the floodwall," Walsh told reporters and local leaders gathered in front of the floodgate on a gray and breezy afternoon.

"There's been speculation that someone might try to blow up the wall. Do you take that seriously?" asked Connor.

"Not really. I've never known of one to be bombed. The only levee explosion I know about was in May 2011 when the Corps blew up a two-mile section of the Birds Point earthen levee in Southeast Missouri to avoid a levee breach across the river at Cairo, Illinois."

"So, there is no chance you would consider blowing the levee again downstream to take pressure off the Elmwood wall?" Connor asked.

"Not a chance. I believe we would have Congress to answer to if we did that."

"You're right," chimed in U.S. Rep. Frank Rogers, whose sprawling congressional district extended from just south of St. Louis to the Arkansas line. "We don't need another blast. What we need is more and stronger levees, not fewer. I have asked for federal dollars to repair the Elmwood wall and hope Congress will approve such funding in the next session."

"Congressman, do you think the floodwall is at risk of sabotage and, if so, from whom?" Connor asked.

"I think our whole levee system is under attack, not by Mother Nature, but by crazed environmentalists, people like the Sierra Club. They would love to tear them all down and kill our economy. But I won't let them do that."

Conner followed up. "Are you saying the wall could be in real danger in Elmwood?"

"I'm not predicting such a dire situation, but if someone wants to damage the wall, I expect it would be a radical environmentalist who would like to turn Elmwood and every city along this great river into a floodplain. That's total nonsense," the congressman said as local officials and community leaders looked on in agreement. Blow up levees and floodwalls? Unthinkable.

But Connor wasn't so sure. At least, he considered, someone may very well be plotting to blow up Elmwood's floodwall.

From the back of the crowd, Tanner Holloway, dressed in a "Save the River" sweatshirt shouted a question to the congressman.

"Rep. Rogers, last time I checked, you are no hydrologist. You have no clue about flooding. Why should government continue to bail out developers who turn floodplains into commercial centers and are then surprised when their developments sustain flood damage?"

Rogers looked flustered, not expecting to field such a question. "You are mistaken," Rogers said, recovering his self-assurance. "We are not living in the 18th century. We are living in the 21st century. Without floodwalls, our whole economy and our way of life would suffer irreparable damage."

"You don't get it, Congressman. What you and the Corps are prescribing will only lead to more disastrous flooding."

"You're wrong," shouted Rogers. "You're dead wrong."

An embarrassed Walsh quickly shut down the debate. "I believe this concludes the news conference. My staff and I have a helicopter waiting back at the airport. We have to get back to Memphis," he stated.

With that, Walsh and Rogers shook hands with the mayor and other dignitaries and headed to a waiting car.

Connor saw Tanner walking briskly away. He ran to catch up.

"You were hard on the Corps and the congressman," said Connor.

"I just said what needed to be said. Officials at all levels of government continue to drink the same Kool-Aid and ignore the reality of walling off our rivers."

"So, blowing up floodwalls is the answer?"

"I didn't say that."

"Well, it would be one solution, even if traumatic."

"Yeah, I guess you could say that. Of course, America's floodwalls and levees are aging. Without major repairs, many of them may fail in the next 10 years."

"And federal, state and local governments probably would just rebuild them," replied Connor.

"You're probably right. And that would be unfortunate. When will people wake up? Walling off the nation's rivers will only exacerbate future flooding and put more people in harm's way."

"Blowing up a floodwall would put people in harm's way too," said Connor.

"Yes. All the more reason why we shouldn't build these walls in the first place."

Connor said goodbye and walked back toward the floodgate and those singing the praises of reinforced concrete barriers.

It struck him that community leaders embraced the floodwall in the same way that kings viewed their fortified castles, a way to protect their way of life.

The trouble was, castles could be breached and floodwalls too. In Elmwood, that could be a disaster, worried Connor.

CHAPTER SIXTEEN

Elroy was working in his Iris garden when police came to his two-story brick home with a wrap-around porch on the city's west side.

About a dozen officers in all, including detectives, uniformed officers and crime technicians, showed up, led by the police chief.

Elroy's wife, Martha, answered the doorbell. Dressed in an old pair of jeans and a sweatshirt, she had not been expecting company on this nice spring day.

"We have a warrant to search the house and Elroy's city hall office," Blair told Martha.

"This is outrageous. Haven't you all done enough damage, bullying by husband and making him out as some type of criminal? You all are despicable," she said, staring coldly at Blair and his men.

"Where is Elroy?"

"He's out back, tending his Irises. I'll let him know the Gestapo is here," she replied stiffly.

Martha walked down the hall, past the large kitchen and out the back door. "Elroy, the police are here."

"What do they want?"

"They have a warrant to search the house and your office at city hall. Blair's heading up the search."

Elroy's face turned red with anger. "The chief has to go. What a jerk," he said, taking off his gardening gloves.

He stared lovingly at his colorful, bearded Iris plants, which even in early April were already displaying a tapestry of purple, blue, white, yellow and maroon. It was mid-morning and the forecast called for temperatures to top out in the mid-60s. A perfect spring day shattered by that bastard Blair, the mayor thought.

He marched back into the house and to the front hall where Blair was standing, along with his officers.

"I see you have come to persecute me," Elroy told Blair.

"Not at all. I am merely serving a search warrant in connection

59

with the murder of your nephew."

"Let me see it," said Elroy, grabbing the warrant from Blair's hand. "Can't believe you got a judge to sign this crap."

"Well, it's legal so let us get to work."

"Be my guest. You won't find anything here. I told you I didn't shoot my nephew."

"If so, Elroy, you don't have anything to worry about."

Blair directed officers to search every room in the house Soon, the house was full of noise as officers opened drawers and cabinets and sifted through cooking utensils. They looked under couch cushions and in bedroom drawers. They went over every inch of his home office, pulling out desk drawers and rifling through his personal files.

Elroy and Martha watched in shock and anger. Elroy wished Blair would drop dead, right there in his living room. It would serve him right.

As the search continued, Blair called Adam on his cell phone. Adam answered as he pulled his unmarked Police Interceptor SUV into the city hall parking lot. "You're good to go," Blair said. "The warrant's been served."

"Will do," replied Adam as he exited the vehicle and walked quickly toward the rear entrance of city hall with a copy of the search warrant in his hand.

He had phoned ahead, informing city manager Don Ritter that police intended to search Elroy's city hall office.

Ritter had unlocked the mayor's office and retreated back to his own office. He didn't want to be involved in any way.

As city manager, he hired the police chief and other department heads. But the city council hired the city manager.

As Ritter saw it, he was stuck in the middle between the chief and the mayor. Either way, he could lose.

Adam entered the mayor's office. It was a small space at the end of the main hallway on the building's first floor.

The room's white walls were covered with framed photographs of the mayor with current and past Missouri governors, congressmen, state lawmakers and council members. Everywhere he turned, Adam saw Elroy's smiling face.

Unlike the search of the mayor's house, Adam was handling

this search solo. Blair wanted it that way. Adam was the department's best detective. If anyone could find crucial evidence like a murder weapon, Adam could. The detective wouldn't miss a thing. If there was evidence to be found, Blair knew Adam would find it.

Adam put on a pair of gloves and began by searching through a long row of metal file cabinets full of city paperwork. He checked each file drawer carefully. He knew the chief hoped he would find the murder weapon. Adam, however, was doubtful. For one thing, he didn't believe the mayor was a murderer.

He finished searching the file cabinets before turning his attention to the large wooden desk that dominated the room. It had a center drawer and two file drawers on either side.

The center drawer had little in it, a letter opener, several pens and pencils and an appointment book. Unlike the city manager and department heads, Elroy preferred to write down his appointments rather than store them on his city computer, which was open atop his desk.

A few newspapers and copies of the Missouri Municipal League magazine were stored in the bottom drawers on the left side of the desk. The right-side drawers were filled with used and unused yellow legal pads, several ties, deodorant and a bottle of cologne.

Buried in the bottom drawer, beneath a stack of legal pads, he found an unloaded, semi-automatic pistol, a Colt 1911 style pistol, the same make used in the killing of Billy Moss.

Adam was stunned. The mayor had told police he no longer owned such a weapon, yet here it was. It might not be the murder weapon. Ballistic tests would determine that. But one thing was for sure, Elroy's life was about to get worse, Adam knew.

He carefully removed the Colt pistol and placed it into an evidence bag, which he signed and sealed. Then he phoned Blair.

"Find anything?" asked Blair upon answering.

"Yes. I found a pistol, right model."

"Good work. Let's get it sent to the state crime lab. See if it is the murder weapon."

"Are you going to arrest Elroy now?"

"No, I want to get the lab results first. Elroy's not going anywhere. If the state crime lab ballistic tests confirm it is the murder weapon, then we'll arrest him. Let's not mess up here. We need to do everything by the book."

After finishing the conversation, Blair watched as his officers finished searching the house. They found nothing.

As officers filed back out of the house, Blair had parting words with Elroy, who yelled at the chief, accusing him of law enforcement malpractice.

"You'll be hearing from my attorney. I'll sue you for all your worth and then some." Blair smiled calmly, turned around and walked out the door. He felt certain the case soon would be solved. The city would need a new mayor.

CHAPTER SEVENTEEN

It was late April before police received ballistic test results from the busy crime lab. Tests confirmed the gun recovered from Elroy's desk was the murder weapon.

Blair decided to make the arrest himself, barely concealing his excitement.

Mid-morning, he showed up at city hall. Elroy was online, on the Carnival Cruise line website. He and his wife had an anniversary coming up. He was thinking of booking a cruise to celebrate.

Elroy looked up and scowled as the police chief walked in. "My day was looking up until you showed up," he said.

"Well, I am afraid it's going to get worse. Elroy, I am arresting you for the murder of Billy Moss."

Elroy jumped to his feet. "You're nuts."

"No, we found a pistol in a desk drawer in this office. Ballistic tests show it was the murder weapon."

"That's impossible. I don't own a pistol now. If you found one, then I'm being framed."

"That's for a jury to decide. I am taking you in. You have a right to remain silent…."

"I know my rights," Elroy interrupted. "Let's get this over with."

Blair led him out in handcuffs to his unmarked car, passing by city employees wide eyed at the sight of the mayor in custody.

Connor was typing away on his computer, working on another flood story when Adam called him.

"Here's a tip for you. The mayor has just been arrested for the murder of Billy Moss."

Connor almost dropped the phone. "Wow. I never figured that. Is there any evidence he did it?"

"We found the murder weapon. It was in his office at city hall."

"Kind of convenient, isn't it?"

"Yeah. I know, it doesn't add up. But it doesn't look good for Elroy. He's being held in the city jail now, but I figure he will bond out soon."

"Thanks, Adam, I owe you."

"You sure do," he replied.

Connor told his editor the news. Lansmon almost spilled an entire cup of coffee. "Damn, that's huge. Let's get it posted online as breaking news as soon as possible," he told Connor.

Connor wrote up a brief story, citing an anonymous source before heading to the police station. By the time he entered the station and spoke to the desk sergeant, Elroy had already bonded out.

"That was quick," he commented to desk Sgt. Rick Meriwether.

"Yeah. Well, Judge Fisher released Elroy on his own recognizance, said he didn't pose a threat to society and wasn't a flight risk."

"He's probably right. If I know Elroy, he'll want to clear his name." But Connor couldn't imagine how the mayor would do it when police had the murder weapon and had tied it to him.

Back in the newsroom, Connor called the mayor's cell phone, but there was no answer. He couldn't blame Elroy.

The police finally put out a brief news release on the arrest, emailing it to area news media and advising them of a 2 p.m. news conference at the police station.

A crowd of reporters awaited the police chief that afternoon. Even some TV crews from St. Louis showed up.

Blair was dressed in full uniform for the occasion. "Thanks for coming. I would like to inform you that my department arrested Elroy James, mayor of Elmwood, this morning on a charge of first-degree murder. He was at his city hall office when he was taken into custody. He has since been released on his own recognizance. He is scheduled to make a court appearance tomorrow."

"There are reports that police have recovered the murder weapon. Can you comment on it?" Connor asked.

"We have recovered a semi-automatic pistol. That is all I am at liberty to say right now."

"But you would not have arrested him without solid evidence?"

"That is correct, Connor. Any other questions, you'll have to talk to the prosecutor. The case is in his hands now."

The main courtroom in the county courthouse in Elmwood was packed the next day with news media and interested residents for Elroy's court appearance.

Judge Fisher gaveled the hearing to order, admonishing those in the audience to be quiet. "Any outburst, and I will have the bailiff remove you from the courtroom."

Elroy was dressed in a dark blue suit, white shirt and American flag tie. His hair was smoothed back. His hands shook as he sat at the defense table, alongside his attorney, Rush Johnson.

Rush, who was in his late 40s, was dressed in an expensive Italian suit, purple silk shirt and a purple bow tie. He was the best lawyer in Elmwood and the most high priced.

"Your honor," Rush began after the charge was read. "My client is one of the most outstanding citizens of this community. As mayor, he has devoted his life to helping this town."

"That's all well and good, but how does your client plead?" the judge asked.

"Not guilty," shouted Elroy.

"Thank you, Mr. James. There is no need to shout. I can hear just fine."

"Judge," resumed Rush, "I would like to state that the prosecution has no basis for this arrest. They have not shown motive. We want the charge thrown out immediately."

"That won't happen, Mr. Johnson. This isn't the time to argue your client's innocence."

Judge Fisher set a new court date. Fifteen minutes after the hearing convened, it was all over. Outside the courtroom, reporters gathered around Rush, peppering him with questions: "Is the mayor innocent? What about the gun?"

"My client did not kill his nephew. As for the gun, clearly someone planted it in the mayor's office. Police found no fingerprints on the weapon. If it had been Elroy's it would stand to reason his fingerprints would have been found somewhere on the Colt pistol. There were no such prints. My client looks forward to clearing his name. We will have no further comments at this time."

With that, Rush ended the impromptu news conference and ushered out the mayor who had been standing behind him.

Ten minutes later, Connor was seated in the prosecutor's office, asking him about the case.

Prosecutor Richard Lamb was not a happy man. For one thing, he disliked reporters. Talking to Connor was the last thing he wanted to do, but the case was already shaping up as a circus and he hoped to keep the media from sensationalizing it.

"The defense attorney said you don't have a motive. Is that true?"

"The prosecution does have a motive, but I am not going to go into that now."

"Does it have anything to do with the floodwall threat?"

"I'll just say Alligator Alley customers heard him threaten the victim. You have already reported that. I don't have anything to add right now," said Lamb as he ushered Connor out and retreated back into the privacy of his office, slamming the door.

CHAPTER EIGHTEEN

Connor worked late the next day. So did Rachel. Both reporters covered night meetings – Rachel, a school board session and Connor, a city council meeting.

Other reporters had gone home by the time both finished their stories and the copy desk signed off on them.

"You hungry?" Connor asked Rachel, who despite a tiring day still looked as fine as ever to him. Connor, on the other hand, was sure he looked like a dead horse.

"I'd love to grab a bite," she said.

They settled on a Mexican restaurant, located a two-block walk from the newsroom. There was a slight breeze which ruffled her hair. Connor thought it made her even more enticing.

The waiter seated them at a corner table. Rachel ordered Carnitas, served with rice, beans and guacamole. Connor had chicken Chimichanga with lots of guacamole, sour cream and pico de gallo. Both had lime Margaritas on the rocks to wash it down.

"What a day. I'm exhausted," said Connor.

"Me too. What did you think of the publisher's pep talk about how we all need to work harder? Translation, we're not filling the vacant feature reporter position."

"Yeah. Not surprising. Practically every newspaper in this nation has been cutting staff or not filling positions over the past five years. Circulation is down. People would rather get their news free of charge in 30-second sound bites," he grumbled.

"Well, it's a damn shame," she said before moving on to the forecast for more rain in the coming days and the growing flood crisis across the river. East Elmwood residents were stranded on a seemingly smaller and smaller area of dry land. Many residents had fled to safety with family and friends.

"It's a mess for sure," Connor said. "To hear some of them tell it, they'd be better off if our floodwall broke, lowering the water level on their side of the river."

"Speaking of the floodwall, do you still think the threatening message on the wall is tied to Billy's murder?"

"I do. But I don't think Elroy killed his nephew. It seems out of character for him."

"So, if the mayor didn't do it, who did and why?"

"I wish I knew. That professor keeps telling me that floodwalls are bad, but he talks about the issue in a scientific way, not like some environmental terrorist."

Rachel was quiet for a moment, her head cocked to one side. "You know, Connor, maybe you're too focused on the environmental issue. Murders are emotional. Maybe Billy's death was revenge for some past wrong."

"I haven't found anything Billy has done except distribute those Bible verses, and that wasn't his idea. He just saw a way to make a fast buck."

"Well, I mean, revenge might be for something else. Maybe someone is blaming a past flood tragedy on our wall. What if someone died in a past flood?"

"Someone in Illinois?"

"Or Missouri."

"You could be right," observed Connor. "That could generate a lot of hatred."

"It might be worth checking the newspaper archives and see if there have been flood deaths."

"That could be a lengthy search, going back decades," Connor considered.

"True, but there's only one way to find out and that's to do it, and I'll be happy to help."

"Thanks. But right now, I don't want to think about it. I feel like I live in the newsroom. It's depressing."

"Cheer up," said Rachel. "Tell you what, let's make a night of it. You told me once you like jazz."

"You bet."

"Well, let's go hang out at Jello, that little jazz club downtown."

"I don't know. We have to work tomorrow."

"Come on, old man. Don't be a party pooper," Rachel responded, sporting a sly smile. Connor couldn't turn down such an invitation.

They each paid for their own meal and made another short walk toward the floodwall and the jazz club, located in an old brick building on River Street that once was a general store.

Jello wasn't too crowded, not surprising since it was a weeknight. They took seats at one of the small, round tables near the stage.

The band, Soul Shades, was performing Boney James' tune, "Butter," one of Connor's favorites. The saxophonist was doing a good job, playing those silky-smooth notes that James was known for.

Connor ordered two glasses of the House Chardonnay. They were each on their second glass of the wine when Rachel asked him to dance.

It was a slow tune. He wondered if he should decline. But she was already moving her blue-jeaned hips to the sexy sounds of "Hold on Tight." How could he resist. He didn't.

He stood up and grabbed her hands as they moved onto the dance floor. He moved his body closer to her swaying body.

For a minute, he thought maybe he shouldn't. After all, he was far older, and she was his co-worker. He feared an office romance, well not really the romance, but what might come next, the breakup.

But the music sucked him in, and, of course, Rachel's exuberant dancing. He held her close and she responded, moving her body alongside his as they danced to that tune and a dozen more.

He was sweating when they finally sat down. He felt flushed with excitement. He smiled, a little embarrassed, and she smiled back, a look of joy on her face. She ran her hand through her hair and downed the remainder of her drink.

"Getting late, maybe it's time to go," she said swiftly.

"Yeah. It's almost midnight. But I sure had fun."

"Me too," she said. "You're not a bad dancer, Connor. Maybe we should try it again sometime?"

"I'd like that," Connor replied even as he wondered if he was being too hasty. It had turned chilly outside as was often the case in spring. He put his arm around her shoulder as they walked back to the newspaper.

"See you tomorrow," she said as he gave her a brief hug.

"Likewise," he said as he watched her saunter off to her red Mini Cooper.

A few minutes later, he pulled out of the parking lot. "What are you doing? What are you doing?" he said to himself. He knew the answer. He just didn't want to acknowledge it. Not now, maybe later.

CHAPTER NINETEEN

Two days after their close encounter, Connor and Rachel met over souffles for breakfast at Smooth Buns. It wasn't a date. It was a working breakfast. They brought their laptops so they could delve into the newspaper archives, looking for stories about area residents who died in past floods. Connor figured there couldn't be too many who had lost their lives as a result of such flooding.

Connor saw Henry Carter, the local historian, seated by himself at a small table along one wall of the bakery and restaurant reading a Missouri history journal. He waved to the bow-tie-clad Carter, who was eating a large blueberry muffin sprinkled with powdered sugar. Carter smiled and waved back.

They had barely settled into their seats and ordered their food when Oliver and Truman, the eatery's owners, stopped by their table.

"My, two reporters in our establishment at one time. What's the occasion? Are you guys now food critics?" asked Oliver.

"No," said Connor, laughing. Rachel smiled at the two men, who made contrasting fashion statements. Oliver was dressed in his usual casual style, while Truman looked as if he was ready to go to an art exhibition.

"We needed to get out of the office and do some research," Rachel said.

"What kind of research?" Truman asked with a mischievous grin, implying the two reporters were in a relationship.

"No, not that kind of research," Connor replied even as the idea appealed to him. "We're looking at past newspaper stories about people who died in floods."

"How morbid," observed Oliver. "You guys need to get out a little more and enjoy life. All this talk of flood victims is depressing."

"Well, at least you'll get a good meal here," Truman said.

"Bon Appetit," a cheerful Oliver advised before heading back to the kitchen while Truman stopped at another table to greet a customer.

Rachel and Connor turned their attention to the newspaper's archives, searching for online flood stories for the past 10 years. They had decided to confine their searches to a 60-mile radius around Elmwood, figuring that anyone who lived farther away would not be concerned with the floodwall.

When their food came, they took a break. Connor drank black coffee. Rachel had sweet tea.

Two hours later, having finished their breakfast and thoroughly searched on their computers for flood victims, they had come up with two possibilities. One was a Bootheel farmer who drowned after his pickup truck was swept away as he tried to drive across a flood-swollen creek in 2017. The other was a man who drowned after the Corps of Engineers blew a hole in an agricultural levee on the Missouri shore south of Elmwood in 2011 to protect the flood-threatened, impoverished city of Cairo, Illinois.

They decided to cross off the creek drowning because it was the result of a flash flood. The other seemed more promising because it involved Mississippi River flooding although Rachel had her doubts.

"The only problem with the levee blast story is that the levee was blown up by the Corps of Engineers to protect an Illinois city. There would be no reason for Illinois residents to object to that."

"Yeah, well maybe we were looking at it all wrong. If the Elmwood wall had failed, it would have relieved pressure downstream and the Corps would not have blasted the agricultural levee, flooding thousands and thousands of acres of rich farmland."

"Maybe. It's worth a shot," she agreed.

It took Connor a day and countless phone calls to track down the brother of the flood victim. Demetrius Patterson's brother, Darius, drowned when water poured through the exploded levee and roared through the small, black village of Grassley. The town of 147 residents never recovered. It became a ghost town before the heavily damaged houses were razed in 2016.

Demetrius, who now lived in Elmwood and repaired cars, agreed to talk to Connor. The next day, they drove down to the abandoned village site in Connor's red SUV.

The village had been located about 40 miles south of Elmwood. Now, there was nothing left on that acreage off a lonely county road except for the concrete foundations where houses, a gin joint and a general store once stood.

"Grassley was just a little place, but I loved it. It was home for me and my brother and parents. We had aunts and uncles who lived here too. It was a great place to grow up. Nobody bothered us," Demetrius said, casting a sad gaze over the site. "Do you know its history?" he asked Connor.

"Not much. I understand it was a black community."

"Right. It was created in 1931 by eight black families who were given the land by a white Baptist minister who wanted a place for African Americans to live without being subject to the racism found in the white communities."

At age 64, Demetrius had closely cropped, graying hair. He ran his hands across his head as he thought of his childhood. "I was born in '54. We was discriminated against all the time for the color of our skin. Even with integration of the public schools, that didn't change, even through my high school years."

"So, what happened to Darius?"

"The damn Corps told us they would blow the levee that May. They gave us 48 hours to leave. We packed up what we could. Our parents had died the previous year. Darius and I were still living in our parents' house. Darius, he was 55, was the last to leave Grassley. He went around checking all the other houses to make sure no one was left behind."

"And were there any others left behind?"

"No, but he didn't leave, not right away. My brother had a drinking problem. He liked whiskey. Lots of it. He was drinking that night. I know because he called me on his cellphone. Said he was going to sleep it off, but he would leave before the Corps exploded the levee, which was around midnight I believe.

"But he never woke up?"

"No, he woke up. Just not in time. He called me from his cell phone as he prepared to wade to his pickup truck. He said the water was already halfway up the wheels. He apparently managed to drive away, but the county road was covered in water, several feet high, only about 100 yards from the village. It was dark. He probably had no idea the water was that deep. The state patrol later said floodwaters swept his truck off the road and into a ditch. He drowned."

"Do you blame the Corps for your brother's death?"

"Of course, I do. They murdered him just as if they had shot him. If Grassley had been a white community, we would have been okay. Doubt the Feds would destroy a white town."

"But you all had flood insurance, right?"

"Yeah. We had it, but it didn't help. See the insurance has a clause. It won't pay for man-made flood damage. The government blew up the levee, not God. So, we got nothing. We all were left on our own. Some people were left with nothing, but Social Security to live on. It was a damn shame and still is."

"I'd be upset if that happened to me and my family," said Connor.

"Yep. So why do you want to know about all this now?" asked Demetrius.

"Well, as you may know, the Elmwood mayor has been charged with a murder in a case which may be connected to a threatening message left on the floodwall. Some people think the mayor is innocent and that the killer may want to blow up the floodwall."

"Whoa. What's that got to do with me? You think I'd want to blow up the wall. Hell, no."

"I'm not suggesting that. But it's true that had the flood breached the Elmwood wall, it would have lowered the water level downstream, making it likely the Corps never would have blown up the levee protecting Grassley."

"Yeah, well I have nothing against levees. Personally, there needs to be more of them."

"Well, some people don't see it that way. They would prefer more unrestricted floodplains."

"Then, maybe you ought to be suspecting some environmental do-gooder rather than this black man. Why is it that you people always want to blame the black man? I think we are done here," said Demetrius, angrily stomping back to Connor's SUV.

They drove back to Elmwood largely in silence. Demetrius scowled, unhappy with Connor's questioning. Connor dropped him off at his south-side home. Demetrius slammed the door as he got out.

Connor watched him walk away. He could picture him being violent. Demetrius had a lot of anger. Still, he concluded, Demetrius didn't seem to want to destroy Elmwood's wall. He'd have to look elsewhere for a possible suspect even as the Mississippi River continued to rise.

CHAPTER TWENTY

Mayor Elroy James wasn't about to lay low, not when his considerable reputation was at stake. He and his supporters organized a rally in front of the massive, white-columned, brick courthouse.

About 200 family members and friends gathered on a cloudy, breezy spring day in April to demand justice for Elroy, who showed up in sport coat, open shirt and dress pants. A red MAGA hat was perched on his head. A vocal supporter of President Trump, Elroy wasn't above catering to the many Trump fans who resided in the city.

Connor and Rachel came to report on the rally. Tyler was there too, snapping countless images of the public protest. Connor was focused on what Elroy and Elroy's attorney had to say. Rachel had convinced her editor to let her cover the crowd.

Lansmon had been impressed with Rachel's desire to cover the hard-news story. She had more experience covering the schools, but she had a nose for news and an enthusiasm to match. Lansmon couldn't say no.

Rachel waded into the noisy, placard-carrying crowd to get a few quotes. One woman, attired in a peasant blouse and jeans, told her, "Elroy's been a great mayor and there is no way he murdered that boy."

A man, sporting a beer belly covered by a dark blue Trump for President t-shirt, commented, "It's pure politics. Prosecutor's a Democrat. He'd love to convict a Republican like Elroy." Nearby, a woman raised a homemade sign which read, "The System Sucks. Prosecute the Prosecutor."

"You know Elroy is innocent. Someone framed him," the woman told Rachel. "The judicial system has clearly failed us. Charging Elroy with murder, what a travesty."

Uniformed police watched the crowd from a distance, clearly on hand as a precaution against some sort of violence. Rachel thought that was unlikely, given that many of Elroy's supporters were middle-aged or older. Some of them probably had been hippies in their youth, maybe even Vietnam War protestors. But she doubted they'd be capable of much violence now.

The mayor stood in front of the crowd, holding a wireless microphone. Two portable speakers were set up on either side of him in the courthouse plaza. TV and radio reporters congregated up front.

"Thanks for coming," Elroy told the crowd. "What a turnout. As you know I have been unfairly charged with murdering my own nephew. Police and prosecutors in this case are on a witch hunt against me because I won't cater to their shenanigans. It's fake news, that's what they are peddling. I intend to win this fight and reveal what a bunch of hypocrites and conniving con artists they are."

The crowd cheered and clapped as Connor held a digital recorder next to one of the loudspeakers, capturing every syllable. A short distance away from Elroy stood the mayor's flamboyant attorney. Rush Johnson grinned as he observed the protest. Connor walked over and greeted Rush.

"Your client seems to be in rare form today."

"He's just speaking his mind, like he always does," said Rush.

"Typically, defense attorneys don't want their clients to make any public comments."

"True. But in this case, the defendant is a beloved public figure, whose name has been dragged through the mud. He has every right to declare his innocence, not just in a courtroom of lawyers and judges, but in the courtroom of public opinion," insisted Rush.

"I'm not sure the judge or the prosecutor will take kindly to the protest."

"Too bad. The judge didn't issue a gag order and I could care less about what that sleaze bag of a prosecutor thinks."

From a second-floor window, Prosecutor Richard Lamb watched the protest unfold. He shook his head in disbelief. Elroy is making a fool of himself. It won't change the fact he's a murderer, Lamb concluded.

Looking up, Connor saw Lamb. He walked away from the demonstration and headed into the courthouse. He climbed the steps two at a time and hurried down the second-floor hallway. He knocked on the door to Lamb's private office.

Lamb opened the door. "What do you want?"

"Any comment about the demonstration taking place below?" Connor said.

"I'm not going to get in a shouting match with the mayor. But I will say this: No amount of protest will keep me from doing my duty as prosecuting attorney. Unlike the defendant, I will not make my arguments outside of the courtroom. You can quote me on that."

"You can count on it," replied Connor.

The protest soon ended. Elroy shared hugs and handshakes with his supporters. Rachel hung around to get some last-minute comments from the mayor's supporters. Tyler was still shooting photos. He captured images of supporters gathered around the mayor and subsequently packing up their placards and departing the scene. Elroy was besieged by broadcast reporters. He patiently answered questions, even those asked again and again by different reporters. Connor hung back. He waited for the scrum of reporters and videographers to leave. He preferred a one-on-one interview.

Elroy was finally alone. Connor approached him on the plaza. "How do you feel about the support you received today?"

"I'm truly thankful. It makes me want to fight even harder to prove my innocence. I'm Elmwood's mayor and I am not going to let anyone railroad me, especially Lamb, that demon Democrat. He would like nothing better than to get me out of office."

"Well, he seems to think he can prove you murdered Billy."

"His case is weak. It relies solely on finding the murder weapon in my office. But, guess what? My prints aren't on the gun. And they have no good motive. No one who overheard the argument with Billy would ever think of me as a murderer. It was just heated words, not anything sinister. A jury will see that. It will take my side."

The conversation ended as quickly as it began. Both men headed to their cars. Rachel and Tyler already had departed in Tyler's Kia before Connor reached his SUV. Connor climbed in and boosted the volume on his favorite SiriusXM jazz channel as he drove back to the newsroom. One thing Connor knew – this court case was going to be unique. Regardless of the outcome, the mayor would not be silenced.

CHAPTER TWENTY-ONE

Rachel sat at her desk sipping sweet tea before typing her story. Her lead came quickly. "The threat meant nothing. The discovery of the murder weapon in the mayor's office meant nothing too. Supporters of Mayor Elroy James are certain someone framed him and that he had nothing to do with the murder of his nephew," she wrote.

An hour later, she had finished a 16-inch story about the protest. Connor had finished his story too. He left the newsroom for an interview with the public works director regarding the city's ongoing flood fight.

Rachel wondered if she should wait for Connor to return before delving into the archives some more, but she rejected that idea. She had time to go through the clip files. There was no need to wait.

The archives were crammed into a small room off the newsroom. The online files only went back to 2000. Earlier files were paper clippings, cut out by the newspaper's librarian and placed in notecard-size folders by category and/or an individual's name. They were stored in small, metal drawers which covered one wall of the room.

Amy Blanchard was the paper's librarian. Now in her late 40s, she had been employed as the librarian for the past two decades. She was devoted to keeping up with the past, recorded in old newspaper clippings and online. She was content being single and saw no reason to date. Rachel doubted Amy had ever dated anyone.

Amy directed Rachel to several thick clip files titled, "Floods." The files were listed by year. She carted a whole stack of files back to her desk. She began with 1999, figuring she would work her way back to the floods in the 1980s or maybe even the '70s. Stories from those decades had not been added to the newspaper's online archive. They only existed on aging newsprint, the stories folded up and crammed into small paper folders. She searched for news about flood victims.

Clippings from 1999 included articles about two motorists who drowned after they ignored barricades and sought to drive through water covering county roads. Rachel kept looking, searching for fatalities that might be associated with a levee break. She found a 1997 story about a man who was struck by a train in a rural area south of Elmwood. The man had been walking on the tracks because they sat higher than the flooded ground. According to the article, the sheriff surmised the man never heard the train approaching because he was wearing headphones and listening to music. Rachel found no reports of flood fatalities in 1996. She wondered if she would find a local levee break that proved deadly.

She was halfway through a thick file of clippings on the 1995 flood when she found it, a news story about Hamilton Jones, an elderly farmer in the East Elmwood area who had drowned. There were two short stories about the man's death as well as an obituary. If it had happened on the Missouri side of the river, the Journal probably would have paid more attention to it, Rachel reasoned. Deaths in Southern Illinois were less important to the Journal's Missouri readers who comprised the bulk of the subscribers, she concluded.

Jones' drowning was covered in the first article as part of a larger story on flood damage. The second story focused solely on his drowning. Hamilton Jones was 90 when he died, drowning when floodwaters plowed through his aging farmhouse in the middle of the night. Friends and family described him as somewhat of a hippie, his long, white hair tied up in a ponytail. According to the news account, Jones drowned when the Mississippi River topped the earthen levee and the weakened levee then gave way, sending a wall of muddy water across his fields and into his home. The levee bordered his land on all sides. When the water rushed in from the river, the other sides of the levee held, serving as a bowl holding in the muddy water and turning it into a relentless, drowning machine.

Family and friends said they had urged him to move to higher ground because of flooding concerns. But Jones refused to leave the family home, at one point saying the levee would hold, "God willing." The obituary promised a funeral at the East Elmwood Baptist Church. Survivors at the time included a brother, Horatio, as well as unnamed nieces and nephews.

Maybe the brother was still alive, Rachel thought. What if a family member or friend blamed Elmwood's immovable wall for pushing water back against the Illinois levee, causing the breach? Would that be a motive for murder? So many questions. Rachel needed to talk to Connor.

Across town, Connor was asking questions of Elmwood public works director Clay Smith. It was late April. Heavy rains continued to pummel the Upper Midwest, sending a torrent of water down river. The river gauge at Elmwood now stood at 50 feet. Another two feet and the river would top the wall, flooding downtown.

"We're doing everything we can right now," said Clay. "Areas north and south of the wall have been flooded. Residents moved out of the area south of the floodwall as a result of federal flood buyouts in past years. But we still have a number of residents living north of the wall. Their neighborhood is flooded. We have closed streets and ordered evacuations. Police and fire personnel are helping with the evacuations. The Red Cross has set up temporary shelter at the community center."

"What about the floodwall? Will it hold?" asked Connor.

"We hope so. We've never seen such high water. If it doesn't hold, the Mississippi will drown the downtown. We do have pumps in place, but they won't be able to keep up with such a deluge."

"Are you concerned someone may seek to blow up the wall?"

"Not really. I know there has been plenty of public concern, but I can't see that happening. Everyone in Elmwood realizes the importance of that wall."

The interview lasted about 30 minutes. Upon returning to the newsroom and his cluttered desk, Connor barely had time to sit down before Rachel was by his side.

"We have to talk," she said. "I think I may have found our flood victim. Hamilton Jones, 90, died in the 1995 flood on his farm across the river when the levee broke."

"Did he have any relatives in the area?"

"A brother, some nieces and nephews. Not sure if any of them are still around here."

"Well, I know who we could ask. Harvey Winston, East Elmwood's mayor. He knows just about everybody over there."

Connor and Rachel wasted little time traveling over to Illinois. The highway was still closed due to high water. The bridge was barricaded on the Illinois side. Connor parked his SUV near the barricade and he and Rachel walked east toward the high water. The flood fight was in full swing. National Guard troops were stacking another wall of sandbags in an effort to save the town from the watery onslaught. Residents and volunteers had turned the strip club into an operations center and shelter. The club's parking lot looked like a lake. The club itself sat on higher ground, but just barely. Floodwaters had closed to within feet of Club Mardi Gras. Sandbags had been stacked around the concrete-block building as protection against flood damage.

People were coming and going across flooded streets in boats and kayaks. Some simply waded through the murky water. Connor and Rachel saw Harvey. At 66 years of age, he was still in good shape physically. He was lifting and stacking sandbags, along with a crowd of other volunteers. "You come to help?" he asked.

"Not exactly," said Connor. "We wanted to ask you about Hamilton Jones?"

"Wow, that's a name from the past. Why do you want to know about Hamilton?"

"We discovered he drowned in the flood of '95," replied Rachel.

"It was terrible. I remember it. The river topped the levee protecting his farm and ultimately collapsed it, sending a wall of water into his home. It happened in the middle of the night. Hamilton had no warning. The river killed him."

"He had a brother. Is he still alive?" asked Rachel.

"No. He died about five years ago. He has some nieces and nephews. Only one of them lives around here, actually on the Missouri side."

"Who is that?" asked Connor.

"Tanner Holloway."

"The college professor?" a surprised Connor asked.

"Yep. That's the one."

"I recently interviewed him. He hates floodwalls."

"He certainly does. Can't blame him," observed Harvey. "If that damn floodwall wasn't here, the Illinois side would fare better. We'd have less chance of levee breaks. As it now stands, our dirt levees can't hold up, not when the water has nowhere to go on the Missouri side thanks to that huge, concrete barrier."

A sweating Harvey paused and looked at Rachel and Connor.

"Are you wondering if Tanner would damage the wall or if he murdered that bartender? You surely can't be thinking that."

"We're just asking questions," said Connor. "We're not accusing Tanner of anything."

"But you're thinking it. And, you're wrong. I've known Tanner for ages. He's not a killer. He may not like the wall, but I've never heard him talk of damaging the wall. He's a college professor, not an eco-terrorist."

But Connor and Rachel weren't so sure. Maybe there was a dark side to Tanner, one fueled by family tragedy.

CHAPTER TWENTY-TWO

Seated at his desk, Connor studied a stack of Journal photos of the 1995 flood compiled by the newspaper's librarian. There were photos showing flood victims being rescued, washed out roads, waterlogged vehicles and damaged homes and businesses. Images of National Guard troops and volunteers piling up sandbags to hold back the water caught his attention. So did the many structures buried in floodwater. One in particular stood out – floodwaters covering all but the roof of an old farmhouse.

"I've seen this somewhere before, I just can't remember where," said Connor, showing the 8 by 10 photo to Rachel who was hovering near his desk, eyeing the stack of flood photos.

"Maybe you saw it at city hall, in the mayor's office," suggested Rachel.

"No. It wasn't at city hall. City officials prefer chamber of commerce images, not those showing destruction in their community."

"We need to talk to Tanner," Rachel said.

"I agree. But I don't want to schedule a chat. We should just show up at his college office. Maybe we can catch him off guard."

"Sounds like a plan."

Connor and Rachel agreed to approach Tanner later that day. The forecast called for rain to move in by late afternoon or early evening. They hoped it would hold off until they had an opportunity to chat with Tanner. Angry clouds had rolled in by 4 p.m. as Connor parked his Ford SUV in a crowded, campus parking lot. He and Rachel walked into the science building and down a hall to Tanner's faculty office.

Rachel had checked his class schedule. Tanner's last environmental science class of the day had ended 10 minutes earlier. She figured the professor should be back in his office. Tanner had just settled back into his office chair when Rachel and Connor arrived.

"Well, if it's not the intrepid reporter," Tanner greeted Connor before introducing himself to Rachel. "What can I do for you two?"

"We wanted to ask you about your family," replied Rachel.

"Specifically, we wanted to ask you about your uncle, Hamilton Jones," Connor said.

Tanner stared harshly at the two Journal reporters, his facial muscles tightening. "Why are you asking about my uncle?"

"Because Mr. Jones drowned in the '95 flood on his Southern Illinois farm, right across the river. Water topped the earthen levee and then the levee failed, sending water crashing into his farmhouse," Rachel said.

"I know. It was a terrible tragedy, but that's ancient history. Surely, you are not interested in my family's misfortune."

"Oh, but we are," observed Connor. "You see, by your own view about floodwalls, your uncle might have survived the flood if there had been no wall protecting Elmwood that put pressure on the earthen levee across the river."

"Certainly, the floodwall made things worse for Illinois residents," agreed Tanner. "But I am not sure what you are getting at."

"Well, as you know, a threatening message was left on the floodwall, and Billy Moss was murdered."

"You mean that bartender?"

"Yes. There's some indication that his murder may be connected to that message and that someone might wish to blow up the wall," said Connor.

"That sounds like pure fantasy to me. Besides, the police already arrested the mayor for the murder."

"But it's possible Elroy didn't do it," said Connor.

"So, you're trying to find someone else to pin it on, and you've decided that someone is me," Tanner replied, his voice growing louder.

"Weren't you angry about the death of your uncle?" asked Rachel.

"Of course, I was. There was no way that levee could have held up to the rising river. It wasn't a reinforced concrete wall. It was an earthen levee, and it wasn't tall enough to hold back such high water."

"I can imagine you might have wanted to take revenge by blowing up the floodwall," Rachel said.

"You're wrong. I'm not a demolition expert. And I don't have any hatred toward Elmwood residents. I live in this town now. No, my anger is toward the Army Corps of Engineers. The Corps for decades has focused on protecting Elmwood from floods, but not the folks across the river in Illinois."

"How so?" asked Connor.

"East Elmwood officials for years and years have pleaded with the Corps to design a stronger, bigger levee for flood protection. But the Corps has no interest in spending money to protect rural Illinois folks," said Tanner.

"But I thought you hated floodwalls?" questioned Connor.

"I do, but I also don't believe my uncle and others in the East Elmwood area should be sacrificed to protect another community."

"Well, can you think of anyone who might want to destroy the floodwall?" asked Connor.

"You might take a look at Harvey Winston."

"You're suggesting East Elmwood's mayor might want to blow up the wall?"

"Absolutely," said Tanner. "Harvey thought of my uncle as kind of a father figure. He adored Hamilton. On top of that, floods have wreaked havoc on East Elmwood, his hometown. He might do anything to try to save it."

"That's interesting," said Rachel. "But at his age, I can't see Harvey committing such a crime."

"That old coot is in better shape than people half his age. You saw him lifting those sandbags," Tanner said.

"You have a point," agreed Rachel. "Still, I can't see him as a murderer."

"I agree. I think Elroy James killed that bartender. Police wouldn't have arrested him, and the prosecutor wouldn't have charged him if they didn't have a case."

"Someone could have framed him," argued Connor.

"You've been reading too many mystery novels. In real life, when you find the murder weapon in someone's office that person is most likely the killer," Tanner said, waving his hands at them, suggesting the interview was over.

Connor and Rachel rose to leave. As they turned their backs to Tanner, they saw the poster-size photo of floodwaters covering all but the roof of a farmhouse. They'd seen it before, back in the newsroom. Connor pointed to the image as he turned back toward Tanner.

"That's a photo of your uncle's farmhouse from then 1995 flood, the place where he died, right?"

"That's correct. You know why I have it here? To remind me of the horrors of Mississippi River floods and how much worse they are because of the folly of man. And you can quote me on that."

CHAPTER TWENTY-THREE

A day after their conversation with Tanner, Rachel and Connor traveled to East Elmwood in search of Harvey Winston. They found the mayor in his office at city hall, a metal-sided building that housed both city offices and a large garage to store the town's one dump truck, an aging fire truck manned by volunteers and a bucket truck. The village used to have a police car. Five years ago, the city sold it after its city marshal, the town's only police officer, retired.

The city building sat atop a small rise at the end of a dead-end street. Sandbags had been stacked high around it to protect it from the rising water. Two large, noisy pumps ran nonstop, funneling floodwater through large pipes away from the building. Even with the pumping operation, water still covered the street leading to city hall. The pumps, however, had managed to keep the gravel parking lot from turning into a lake. Harvey's black SUV was parked in front of city hall, along with his aging pickup truck. The SUV was his late wife's vehicle. He preferred to drive the pickup truck, which he usually stored in his garage at night. The SUV seldom left its parking space at city hall. The mayor thought of it more as a remembrance of his wife Frannie rather than something to actually drive. Still, from time to time, he drove it, mostly when he wanted to be alone and away from the public's prying eyes. Driving either vehicle was a challenge these days, particularly when he traveled to Elmwood. He had to drive slowly through floodwaters, keeping to the middle of the roadways as best he could and navigating through the roadblock at the Illinois entrance to the bridge.

When Connor and Rachel arrived, Harvey was wearing an old sweatshirt and jeans muddied by the flood fight. His basset hound, Bobo, rested on a fuzzy brown dog bed in a corner of the office. Bobo looked up eagerly at the visitors, hoping for doggie treats. Seeing none, the black, brown and white floppy eared dog hunkered down in his soft bed. Clearly, there was no reason for him to get worked up about these visitors. Harvey was talking on his cellphone when Rachel and Connor arrived. He was requesting more sandbags and pumps from the Illinois National Guard.

Rachel and Connor waited patiently while Harvey pleaded for more help. When he hung up, he sighed. "I shouldn't have to beg for help, but that seems to be the only way to get National Guard officials to get off their ass and give us some additional help. You'd think I was asking for the moon."

"Did they agree to your request?" asked Connor.

"Yeah, but only after I pleaded with them for 20 minutes. It's damn frustrating. But I'm sure you're not here to listen to my griping. I assume you are here to see if East Elmwood has drowned yet."

"Well, we do have some questions and it does involve the flood," Rachel said. "We recently talked to Tanner Holloway about the death of his uncle."

"I am sure he had a lot to say."

"Yes, he did. He suggested that you might want to blow up the Elmwood floodwall," Connor said.

"Did he accuse me of murdering that bartender too?"

"No. He said he believes Elmwood's mayor did it," said Rachel.

"Glad he thinks I'm not a murderer. Why would he accuse me of being a potential bomber?"

"He said you thought of Hamilton as a father figure," Rachel replied.

"Well, that's true. My dad died in a car accident when I was a kid. Hamilton was close friends with my father. After dad's death, Hamilton treated me kind of like a son."

"So, did you blame the wall for his death?" questioned Connor.

"In a way, I did. Still, we all knew the earthen levee might fail. I wished Hamilton had moved to higher ground. But he refused to leave the family home, said it was part of his heritage."

"Did Tanner ever tell you how he felt about his uncle's death?"

"Sure. He said he hated the floodwall, blamed it for his uncle's death."

"You think he would really try to blow up the wall?" Connor asked.

"That's hard to imagine. But I do know he would have the knowledge to do it. In college, he worked two summers with the demolition crew at the quarry."

Connor and Rachel glanced at each other, surprised by this new information.

"There's something else," added Harvey, scratching his head. "I've been thinking about this ever since that Moss fellow was shot. Wasn't it a Colt 1911 pistol?"

"Yes, that's right," replied Connor.

"Tanner used to shoot a Colt pistol. It was Hamilton's. He taught the kid how to shoot. Tanner became pretty good at it. He and his uncle used to go to shooting competitions when Tanner was a teenager. Tanner won quite a few of them."

Harvey reached into a bottom drawer of his wooden desk. "I have a picture here somewhere." He rummaged through an assortment of papers and faded photographs, some of them stained with coffee. "Aha, here it is," he said, pulling out an old 5 by 7 inch, black and white photo of Hamilton Jones with his arm around Tanner Holloway, who was holding a first-place trophy at the conclusion of a shooting match.

"Are you suggesting Tanner killed Billy Moss?" asked Rachel.

"I'm not going that far. But I will say, there's no doubt Tanner was right at home with such a pistol. If he were to kill someone, that would be the gun he'd use," said Harvey. "I'm sure of that."

Harvey rose. "I've got to get back to the flood fight," he told them as Bobo looked up with his sad eyes in anticipation.

"You like my dog?" Harvey asked.

"He's cute," said Rachel.

"He keeps me company since my wife passed away from ovarian cancer nearly two years ago. Being mayor can be a lonely job at times. But with Bobo around, I'm not so lonely. Of course, being short legged, he doesn't do well with all this floodwater. I pretty much carry him from the truck to the office to the house. Still, I can't complain," said Harvey, bending down and scratching Bobo's ear before turning back to his visitors.

Connor and Rachel shook hands with Harvey, wished him well with the flood fight and headed toward the door. But as they were leaving, Connor spied a paint can in a corner of the office. A splattering of red paint showed on the lid and down the sides of the can.

Connor nudged Rachel and pointed to the can. "Are you planning something?" he asked Harvey.

90

"Oh, no. Not sure where that came from. With this flood fight, there are a lot of people coming in and out of here – volunteers, emergency personnel, National Guard troops."

Connor approached the can and bent down to take a closer look. The paint was blood red in color, just like the message on the flood-wall. A sliver of paper was visible beneath the can. Connor lifted it. The paper stuck to a dab of paint on the bottom of the can. Connor slowly pealed it off. He turned it over to find a typed message: "Na-hum, 1:8. DROWNING, DROWNING, DROWN."

"What is that?" asked Harvey.

"It's a Bible verse about how we are all going to drown," said Connor. "A bunch of these verses were found around town a while back. Billy Moss admitted he was paid by someone to distribute the verses. A lot of people saw it as a threat to tear down the floodwall."

"That's crazy. You don't think I was behind that?"

"It's certainly strange," said Rachel, "although it does seem un-likely that you would leave the paint can in plain sight if you were the culprit."

"I've got to agree with her," said Connor.

"Take the can. You can give it to the police if you want. I have nothing to hide," insisted Harvey, raising his voice, causing Bobo to bark. "And I sure am too busy trying to save my town to worry about the damn floodwall."

CHAPTER TWENTY-FOUR

Connor sat on a park bench in front of an image of Elmwood's Civil War naval battle on the downtown floodwall mural. The painted scene showed the Union vessel pummeling the Confederate steamboat with heavy cannon fire in the 1861 engagement. The Confederate ship stayed afloat and managed to flee downriver. It wasn't much of a battle, but it was a proud moment to the city leaders of that day. Today, the fleeting river battle was held in high esteem and had its place on the 10-year-old floodwall mural that recounted Elmwood's storied past.

Clouds rolled in and out blocking the sunlight, creating a wave of shadows on the pavement. Twenty minutes after Connor had taken a seat, Adam arrived, sporting coat and tie and his ever-present Glock.

Connor had phoned Adam after he and Rachel returned from their conversation with Harvey.

"What's so urgent?" Adam asked, seating himself beside Connor.

"Rachel and I just got back from interviewing the East Elmwood mayor, Harvey Winston. Guess what we found in his office?"

"I haven't a clue."

"We discovered a can of red paint. A Bible verse was stuck on the outside of the can, where the paint had dripped."

"Are you suggesting it was the same paint as was used on the threatening message on the floodwall?"

"Well, you decide," said Connor, lifting up a plastic bag containing the paint can.

"Hope you didn't destroy any evidence, Connor."

"Me too, although I suspect you won't find any prints on the can, except for mine."

"No doubt, that's right."

"There's another thing we found out. That college professor, Tanner Holloway, had an uncle who drowned in the flood of '95.

And Tanner was a good shot. He won shooting competitions using his uncle's semi-automatic pistol."

"Are you suggesting Mr. Holloway killed Billy and Mr. Winston vandalized the floodwall?"

"It's a possibility. Maybe it wasn't all the work of one man," suggested Connor.

"And what about the stolen dynamite? How does that figure into your plot?"

"Actually, I discovered Tanner worked at the quarry as a college student. He would have had access to the explosives."

"But the dynamite wasn't stolen years ago so it's unlikely Tanner would be the culprit," reasoned Adam.

"Maybe so. Still, he could have done it. He had a motive."

"What motive?"

"Tanner philosophically hates floodwalls. He believes they restrict rivers, leading to higher water levels and more severe flooding."

"Yeah, but it's a long walk from an environmental viewpoint to plotting to blow up the wall. And what about the threatening message on the floodwall? How is that connected to Tanner?"

"I don't know," said Connor. "So far, there is nothing that ties Tanner to the graffiti. But it still doesn't make sense for Harvey to have left that can of paint in his office. Perhaps someone else left it there. It could have been Tanner."

"That's one way of looking at it, except for one thing – a half hour ago, the professor called the police station and reported that someone had dumped red paint all over his Toyota."

Connor's jaw dropped. All his investigative effort seemed to have blown up in his face. Tanner, the victim? He hadn't considered it. And what about Harvey Winston?

"You said you just returned from interviewing Mr. Winston?"

"Yeah."

"If so, Connor, it appears you may have just given him an alibi."

Adam took the bagged paint can and headed for his unmarked police car. "Nice try, Connor. Maybe you should leave the police work to professionals," he said.

"There's something wrong and you know it. Elroy didn't kill Billy, I'm sure of it."

"Well, the prosecutor thinks otherwise. At this point, the police chief is focused on making sure we tie up any loose ends."

Connor watched Adam drive off. He sat on the bench for another half hour, trying to solve the puzzling evidence.In the end, he walked back to the newsroom, huge doubts creeping into his mind. He was stumped as how to proceed or even if he could proceed with his investigation.

Seated at his desk, Connor sorted through his reporter notebooks, looking for notes on his previous conversations with Tanner. Rachel eyed him from her desk. She wanted to ask him about his visit with Adam. But she could tell he was in no mood to talk. He was clearly wrestling with something, mumbling to himself.

Thirty minutes later, he grabbed a new notebook, wrote down an address and rushed out of the newsroom. Connor climbed into his SUV and headed toward an older neighborhood near the college. He soon found what he was looking for, an older, Spanish tiled, brick home with a garage that had been attached at a later date.

It was impossible to miss the black Toyota parked in the driveway. Poured on red paint covered the hood, front windshield and the trunk. The paint matched the color of the threatening message on the floodwall.

Tanner was standing outside, talking on his cellphone, making arrangements to have the vehicle cleaned. Connor parked his car on the street.

Tanner had his back turned to the street and didn't see Connor approach. "Wow, somebody did a number on your car," Connor said.

The professor turned around. He scowled when he saw who it was. Connor stood quietly while Tanner finished talking to the cleanup company.

After finishing that conversation, he turned his attention to Connor. "It's you again. You are becoming a real nuisance."

"I understand you reported the vandalism to police."

"Not that it's any of your business, but yes I did."

"When did it happen?"

"I don't know for sure. I discovered the vandalism about an hour ago. I normally park my car in the garage, but I left it in the driveway because I have a class to teach this afternoon. I planned to run an errand before my class. When I came outside, I saw the paint poured over my car. What a mess."

"It looks like the paint used on the floodwall," Connor said.

"Yeah, well at least I'm off the hook as a suspect. Clearly, you can't blame me for the threatening message. Obviously, whoever vandalized my vehicle is most likely the same person who wrote that message on the wall."

"Could be," said Connor. "Or maybe you poured the paint on your vehicle."

"Why would I do that?" an irritated Tanner asked.

"So people wouldn't think you painted the threatening message. And there's the murder of Billy Moss."

"Are you accusing me of that too?"

"Harvey said you were a skilled marksman as a teenager. Your uncle let you shoot his Colt pistol, the same kind of weapon used to kill Billy."

"You have a real imagination; I'll give you that. But I've told you, I'm not a criminal. The police have Billy's killer and it's not me. I want you to leave now," shouted Tanner. "And don't come back or I may have to file a complaint of harassment."

"I just thought maybe you could clear up the mystery," said Connor, seeking to continue the conversation.

"Elroy James killed the bartender. The police and prosecutor say so. As for the floodwall message, maybe Mr. James did that too. I'm confident the police will figure it out. You need to quit playing detective. You're clearly not a good one, and you have no right to threaten me with your ridiculous suspicions. Get lost or I'll call the police," Tanner yelled.

Connor did not reply. He walked back to his Ford Escape, having clearly unnerved Tanner. But was Tanner guilty? After all, thought Connor, an innocent man might behave just like Tanner. He found it hard to believe Tanner would pour paint on his polished Toyota. And what about Harvey Winston? Could he be plotting to blow up the wall? More questions, no answers. It was driving Connor crazy.

CHAPTER TWENTY-FIVE

From the air, the Mississippi River looked like a muddy ocean, running to the horizon. Connor observed the watery landscape from a National Guard helicopter with Corps of Engineers Maj. Gen. Ted Walsh.

Twenty-four hours after his latest interview with Tanner, Connor was getting a bird's eye view of flooding along the river. Tyler accompanied him, snapping photo after photo from a Nikon outfitted with a long, zoom lens.

From the sky, the flood disaster facing East Elmwood was easy to see. The village looked like a small island in danger of washing away any minute. Houses and the few businesses there were hidden behind walls and walls of sandbags. The town's streets looked more like small rivers. Boats plied the flooded roads. Residents, who could, parked their vehicles on the dry pavement afforded by the Mississippi River bridge.

On the Missouri side, floodwaters covered areas north and south of the wall. Fortunately, for many residents north of the wall, the rising topography kept their homes largely dry even as their yards became swamps. But south of the wall, now mostly bare ground as a result of past flood buyouts, the area resembled a wild marsh.

From the helicopter, Elmwood's concrete wall looked like a thin, penciled, fragile line. Connor questioned if the wall could hold up to the enormity of the flood.

The waterway was devoid of barge traffic, the U.S. Coast Guard having shut down river traffic weeks ago because of swift current and in an effort to put less strain on levees.

Walsh pointed to Elmwood's wall. The muddy river stood at 50 and a half feet on the gauge, less than two feet from the top of the wall. "We hope it holds, but we've never seen the water this high before. Plus, there's the issue of an aging wall that needs to be reinforced. Congress has yet to provide us the funding we have requested."

"Is there anything you can do to guard against the wall failing?" asked Connor.

"At this stage, not much other than prayer."

"As you know, there's concern about possible sabotage. Have you considered that possibility?"

"Not really. The Corps is more concerned with natural flooding. It's the job of law enforcement to worry about criminal activity."

"But you do concede that if the wall fails, it would be a huge disaster."

"Absolutely," the major general said. "And very likely we would be facing loss of life in addition to millions and millions of dollars in damages to buildings, streets, sewers and water lines."

"So far, you have ruled out blowing a hole in the Birds Point agricultural levee south of here, like you did some years ago. Are you rethinking that?" asked Connor.

"Not at this time."

"But you might at some point?"

"Yes, if we feel the wall is close to being breached. It would be an option. We're hoping the water starts receding soon. If not, we could have a major problem."

The aerial tour of the flooded area ended 40 minutes after it started. By the time Connor and Tyler arrived back in the newsroom, Connor was already thinking about the wall and the missing dynamite.

"How did it go?" asked Rachel.

"It was terrifying."

"The helicopter ride?"

"No, the scope of the flooding. East Elmwood looks like it could float away any minute. And our floodwall looks inadequate to hold floodwaters at bay. There just simply is too much water. Any kind of breach of the wall would be devastating."

"Oh, by the way, Lansmon has been in a meeting in the publisher's office with the police chief for an hour now. Not sure what it's about, but Lansmon had a sour look on his face before he entered the meeting," Rachel told Connor.

"Who knows? Any meeting involving the publisher irritates Lansmon." Publisher Dan Steele was in his early 40s. Having taken over from his father, who bought the paper decades ago, Steele was faced with declining subscription and ad revenue. His solution had been to cut staff and pay the remaining newsroom staff as little as possible.

Connor and Rachel had barely finished their conversation when Lansmon strode into the newsroom and signaled for them to come to his office. Framed images of the "Shoe" comic strip adorned the walls, including one where the editor was chopping up a story. Lansmon's desk was covered in paperwork. The Washington Post website was called up on his computer.

Lansmon instructed them to sit down around a small conference table. He sat down too.

"I just spent over an hour with Dan and that pompous police chief, who berated us for questioning Tanner Holloway and treating him like a murder suspect and someone who might want to blow up the floodwall."

"Wow. We must have hit a nerve," Connor said, grinning.

"Yeah, well, Dan made it clear to the chief that we will not be bothering Mr. Holloway anymore. We are supposed to leave it up to law enforcement and the prosecutor. If they see fit to further investigate Mr. Holloway, they will."

"Are you taking us off the story?" asked Connor.

"Yes, for now."

"But I believe we were making headway," Rachel said. "What's wrong with asking questions, particularly in light of comments by Harvey Winston?"

"What's wrong is that the police chief is bitching about it and Dan is buying it. It's my ass if you 'harass' Tanner. That's Dan's word, not mine. For now, lay off Tanner. You've got plenty of other stories to write."

"I can't believe we are being policed over our investigation," Connor said.

"Well, believe it. And listen carefully, I don't want to hear any more about it. Not one word. Got it?" he said, giving a long look at Connor and Rachel.

Rachel smiled and nodded her head. Connor mumbled to himself. The two reporters quietly left Lansmon's office and returned to their desks.

"What crap," said Connor, collapsing into his chair. Rachel

stopped at his desk and looked at Connor with amusement.

"Don't you get it?" she asked.

"Get what? Lansmon told us he didn't want to hear any more about it. He didn't tell us we couldn't pursue leads. He just doesn't want to know about it."

"Good point. But we still can't question Tanner again without risk of getting called on the carpet again."

"We can work around Tanner. He's not confiding in us anyway. Let's look for another way to peel back this mystery," suggested Rachel.

"You're right. From now on, we'll just have to be more discreet," observed Connor.

They got to work, focusing their attention on other news. Rachel wrote about therapy dogs in an elementary school and Connor produced an article about the poor condition of city hall and suggestions by city officials to float a bond issue to replace it.

But the investigation was never far from their minds. By the end of the day, they wanted to talk about it again and satisfy their hunger.

They decided to grab a bite at Alligator Alley. Connor ordered a catfish po'boy and seasoned fries. Rachel chose shrimp etouffee and a house salad.

They initially talked about the investigation and how to proceed. Connor decided to follow up with his friend, Adam, to see if he might have a new lead, particularly regarding the theft of the quarry dynamite. Rachel volunteered to talk to strip-club owner Marissa Hue. Maybe she could shed some light on Harvey Winston and the possibility he might be involved in some way. After all, both Tanner and Harvey knew each other, and both knew Hamilton Jones. Maybe they were working together and suggesting each other as a suspect might have been intentional, she suggested.

Despite their commitment to the investigation, they soon tired of the shop talk. It felt like they were on a never-ending treadmill.

"I wish I could focus on something besides the wall," observed Connor between gulps of a cold mug of beer.

"Me too," agreed Rachel, sipping a glass of house red wine.

"You know, maybe we could put our work aside one of these evenings," suggested Connor.

"Connor, are you asking me out?" she asked, flashing a beguiling smile at him.

"Well, yeah. I guess I am," he said. "Maybe this weekend. We could go to the free concert in the Elmwood City Park and then grab a bite to eat."

"Sounds good. I'll put it on my busy schedule," she said with a laugh. Connor laughed too, nice and easy. She had that effect on him.

CHAPTER TWENTY-SIX

Marissa Hue was a short woman with long black hair. Her parents had immigrated to Southern Illinois from Vietnam when she was a baby. She had no memory of Vietnam, but she embraced her parents' past. She loved to wear Vietnamese-crafted necklaces with blue jeans, cotton blouses and sandals.

She wore a silver and jade necklace when she met one morning with Rachel in Club Mardi Gras, which was still serving as a base of operations for the flood fight in East Elmwood. Sandbags surrounded the building and, so far, floodwaters had not entered the masonry structure.

Marissa was sitting on the edge of the circular stage, which in normal times would have showcased breast-showing, G-stringed dancers all night long. During the flood fight, it had become a storage area for work coats, gloves, shovels, towels, emergency lights and other items.

Rachel boated over a flood-covered road to reach the strip club. Marissa greeted Rachel with a firm handshake and a warm smile.

"I understand you want to talk to me about Harvey," said Marissa.

"Yes. We were looking for some background on your mayor, who seems to have the energy of a much younger man."

"Yes, he does. He has been leading this flood fight for some two months now. The flooding seems endless. I can't believe the river has yet to crest. It's awful."

"So, is Harvey originally from East Elmwood?"

"Yes. He grew up here. He loves the community. From your side of the river, Ms. Short, you may think East Elmwood isn't much to look at. But the people here are wonderful. We help each other out."

"I assume he is retired," observed Rachel.

"Yes. He's had various careers. He ran a small grocery store and then a hardware store. Both of those went bankrupt years ago, not enough customers to make it work. He subsequently worked as an insurance agent before retiring at the end of last year."

"How long has he served as mayor?"

"About 10 years I think," said Marissa. "Before that, he served, on the council. He was always volunteering his time, heading up food drives and coaching youth baseball. He was always on the go, and still is. Oh, and I believe he served in the Army for a few years right out of high school. He was stationed over in Germany. When he left the Army, he came home and married his high school sweetheart."

"Having been in the Army, I guess he knew a lot about firearms?"

"Oh, sure. He had a huge collection of handguns—pistols, I believe. I really didn't pay much attention to it. I think he got rid of most of his handguns a few years ago. Seems like he told me that."

"You own a gun?"

"I've got a Beretta, but most of the time it stays in a drawer in my office. I pay a lot of money to off-duty cops to keep my club safe for both customers and my employees. I don't need to pack a gun. Still, I like having the Beretta in my office, just in case."

"Did you ever hear Harvey say he wanted to blow up the floodwall?"

"Not like that. I mean we all feel Elmwood's floodwall has made flooding worse for us, but I've never heard him make any serious threat."

"So, he's not the angry type?"

"Good Lord, no. I mean he might raise his voice sometimes out of frustration, but never in a menacing way."

"Do Harvey and that college professor hang out together?"

"You mean Tanner?"

"Yeah."

"Not really. Tanner grew up here, but he lives across the river now. Tanner has been over here a lot, helping with the flood fight. So, Harvey and Tanner have seen a lot of each other, but not socially. They run in different circles."

"How so?"

"Well, Tanner is an academic sort, a respected faculty member at Elmwood College. Harvey is more down-to-earth. He never graduated from college. He took some classes after he got out of the Army, but he never stuck with it. But that doesn't mean he isn't smart. He knows business stuff. If you ask me, he's an entrepreneur."

"But you said some of his business ventures failed?"

"Right, but it wasn't his fault. It's tough to run a business in a small town like ours."

"Both men knew Hamilton Jones?"

"Oh, yeah. You couldn't live in this area and not know Hamilton. He was kind of a hippie type. Loved the outdoors."

"I hear, Tanner and Harvey were close friends of Hamilton despite the age differences."

"They were. Hamilton was kind of like a father to them. They would do anything for him, but I don't think Tanner and Harvey hung out together much unless they were both visiting Hamilton at his farm. Like I said, they were in different social circles. I think Harvey kind of envied Tanner because people here thought of him as this successful professor, you know, boy from a Podunk town makes good."

Rachel turned the conversation away from Harvey. She didn't want to focus too much on Harvey, afraid Marissa would become reluctant to talk to her.

"How are you coping? I mean, all your businesses, which are the only businesses over here, are shut down."

"It's been tough. I've had to take out a short-term loan to tide me over. I've also opened a club in Cairo. It's just temporary. It's housed in a former fire station. The fire pole is kind of a featured attraction," Marissa laughingly observed. "I needed to serve my customers, make some money and pay my girls. They need the work, and I'm loyal to my employees."

"I'm sure they appreciate that," said Rachel.

"We'll all appreciate it more when this flood is over," said Marissa, "and you guys quit asking us about the floodwall."

CHAPTER TWENTY-SEVEN

Connor sat impatiently at his desk, waiting to hear back from his friend, Adam. He wanted to know if the police detective had uncovered any new information on the college professor or the East Elmwood mayor.

Connor busied himself by tidying up his desk, which consisted largely of moving used reporter notebooks to a bottom drawer. Rachel was across the river, talking to Marissa Hue.

His cellphone beeped loudly. Connor answered it. "What's new?" he asked.

"Did some checking," said Adam. "It appears both Mr. Holloway and Mr. Winston worked at the quarry decades ago. They didn't work there at the same time. You know there is an age difference there."

"Tanner is much younger," Connor observed. "So, did either have access to dynamite?"

"Yes, but the explosives were stolen only about six months ago. Neither man had worked there in decades. Doubtful they would have broken into the place."

"Why do you say that?"

"I checked with the company. The quarry is surrounded by an 8-foot chain-link fence, topped with two feet of razor wire. And there are electronic sensors on the fence. If someone climbed the fence or cut through it, and there is no evidence that happened, an alarm would have sounded."

"So, who stole the dynamite?"

Haven't a clue, but if I had to guess, I'd say it was a disgruntled employee or a recently fired worker. The most obvious way to have removed the dynamite was to hide it on a company truck and drive it right through the gate during working hours. Lots of people work there. Nobody would have paid any attention to a truck coming in and out of the quarry."

"Possibly. But in my mind, Tanner could have stolen the explosives, or maybe Harvey."

"You just don't want to give up on your eco-terrorism theory," Adam said.

"Your boss only seems interested in seeing Elroy convicted. He convinced my publisher and editor to lay off any questioning of Tanner."

"Sorry about that. But Blair doesn't see a need to look for someone else to pin Billy's murder on. He's certain Elroy shot Billy. The evidence so far seems to prove it."

"But, Adam, no dynamite was found in his possession."

"True. But there is no evidence the shooting and the theft of the dynamite are connected."

"So, police don't believe someone wants to blow up the wall?"

"There's no real evidence of that other than the message on the wall," insisted Adam.

"Yeah, the message. Someone left that threatening message. Then you take into account the Bible verses. Based on what Billy said, someone paid him to distribute those verses about flooding. And then Billy was murdered."

"I agree it's suspicious. But we need evidence, Connor. So far, we don't have any evidence to suggest the floodwall is in real danger of being blown up. If you have any solid evidence, call me."

"You can count on it. I'm not giving up."

"I'm not asking you to. But be careful and watch your back. Blair and your publisher are friends. The chief might push for your firing down the road unless you back off questioning Tanner."

"Don't worry. I'm trying to tread lightly, but I won't be bullied by anyone."

"I was just giving you some friendly advice. Take care," said Adam, ending the conversation.

Connor sat quietly at his desk, contemplating his next step. It was clear the police weren't focused on the wall. They weren't focused on the missing dynamite either. Someone stole the explosives, but who and why.

Maybe the first step, he thought, was to figure out how the dynamite was removed from the quarry. If it wasn't driven out on a quarry truck, how was it removed?

That question was still on his mind when Rachel returned from East Elmwood.

"Learn anything?" he asked.

"Yes. Harvey spent a few years in the Army and he had a huge collection of handguns, although Ms. Hue thinks he has sold off the collection."

"Could be the murder weapon was his," said Connor.

"Yeah. She said she thought he collected mostly pistols. And, she said, Hamilton was like a father figure to both Harvey and Tanner. She said Harvey and Tanner weren't really close friends, but knew each other and saw each other at Hamilton's farm on occasion."

"Maybe they are plotting together to blow up the wall," suggested Connor. "The police, however, don't seem concerned."

"You talked to Adam?"

"Yeah. He told me there is no evidence the theft of the dynamite is connected to Billy's murder or the message on the floodwall."

"So, what are we are going to do?"

"We need to figure out how the dynamite was removed from the quarry. Adam seems to think neither Tanner nor Harvey took the dynamite. He said it's more likely that a current employee or recently disgruntled worker took the explosives and drove them out the front gate of the quarry in a company vehicle."

"What about finding a way through the fence?"

"According to Adam, the fence is equipped with sensors. If someone had cut the fence, an alarm would have sounded. And going over the fence would be difficult because it is topped with razor wire. But if Tanner or Harvey did it, or both, they must have found a way around it, and we can do the same."

"How?"

"Well, I've driven by the quarry. The north side of the property abuts a wooded area, which would provide cover for anyone trying to sneak into the quarry."

"But how would they get around or over the fence?"

"That's what we need to find out. You up for a hike through the woods this weekend? The quarry doesn't operate on Sundays. Seems to me, that would be a perfect day to do a little snooping."

"Sounds good to me. I love a good hike and one with a mystery even better," said Rachel, her face lit up with an infectious smile.

"It's a date. I mean...."

"I know what you mean, Connor. I'll wear my hiking boots." Connor nodded his head, embarrassed to speak. An appointment to snoop was nothing like a date. Still, he couldn't help thinking it might be nice to have a picnic lunch.

CHAPTER TWENTY-EIGHT

Friday was busy as always in the newsroom with reporters working on stories for the weekend edition. Rachel buried herself in storytelling, writing about a day in the life of kindergarten students as well as putting together a lengthy piece on a plan by the local public schools to construct an aquatic center.

Connor spent the day writing about plans for a new airport terminal and interviewing state lawmakers about a proposed transportation tax measure.

By the end of the day, both Rachel and Connor were ready to kick back and leave their work behind. They looked forward to the free concert in the park although neither considered it a real date. They thought of it more as just two friends enjoying a good time, at least that's what they told themselves.

The event was one of a series of concerts put on every spring by the Downtown Merchants Association in the tree-shaded city park on a bluff overlooking the riverfront.

Connor provided a blanket, a bottle of semi-sweet red wine and two plastic wine glasses. Rachel brought everything else for the occasion, including a picnic basket with an assortment of cheese, crackers and summer sausage. They came straight from work.

Connor wished he had had time to change. But he hoped he didn't look too ragged. Rachel thought he looked just fine in blue jeans, untucked dress shirt and blue Skechers. Rachel worried she should have gone home and changed. But Connor thought she looked great in her skinny jeans, tight black shirt with rolled up sleeves and black and white checkered tennis shoes. Her thick auburn hair was eye-catching too.

The concerts were popular, drawing hundreds of people of all ages and all walks of life. Whole families attended. The concerts drew everyone from aging civic leaders to millennial computer geeks, bankers to construction workers, retired teachers to coffee-bar owners. Many in the audience brought their dogs.

Connor loved the gatherings. It brought out the best in people, he believed. No pretense. People just enjoying each other's company and the music.

The performers weren't household names. Most were Nashville songwriters who traveled to Elmwood and other cities like it for a little money and the enjoyment of performing.

This concert featured a woman who had grown up in Southeast Missouri before moving to Nashville. She was an accomplished songwriter, having written tunes for a whole host of Country Music stars.

Her own singing was geared more toward Memphis blues. Connor filled Rachel's glass with wine and then poured himself an equal amount.

They sat next to each other on the blue-and-green plaid blanket as they listened to the music. Rachel kicked off her shoes, exposing her bare feet and red-nail-polished toes. Connor smiled as he watched her wiggle her toes.

As the concert wore on, Connor moved closer to Rachel, putting his right arm behind her back. She leaned into him, laying her head on his shoulder. It felt good. The singer/songwriter was belting out a tune from the park's restored gazebo. Connor liked the sad song about a jilted lover, although he was feeling far from sad at the moment. He could feel Rachel's breast against his ribs.

"What a great night," she said, cooled by the spring breeze.

"It sure is," said Connor, who 40 minutes into the concert had all but forgotten about work, about the wall, about Harvey, about Tanner.

Fifty minutes into the concert, Connor kissed the top of Rachel's head. She looked up at him, a soft smile on her face. Connor didn't want the concert to end.

As the concert continued, Rachel stretched out on her side. Connor sat by her, resting his right hand on her thigh. Neither said much as they listened to the music.

The concert ended about an hour and 20 minutes after it started. "That was fun," said Rachel as she and Connor stood up. They retrieved the blanket, picnic basket and the now empty wine bottle.

Connor looked at his watch. It was nearly 8 p.m. "I'm hungry. Want to grab a bite?" he asked.

Rachel nodded. "Sure. We've had the appetizers, now we need the main course." They decided on a local downtown eatery known for its dry-rub ribs.

Adam's Ribs was housed in a small, brick building that once housed a cigar store. The walls still carried the odor of cigars. It added to the dining experience, Connor thought.

The hostess, a young gal who sported purple-dyed hair and a nose ring, seated them at a corner table at the back of the room. Their waitress was a college student with short, black hair and green fingernails. Connor and Rachel ordered Memphis baby-back ribs and water. They talked about the concert, the weather and just about anything else, outside of themselves. Neither talked about work, especially their investigation.

"It's been a nice night," said Rachel.

"I was thinking the same thing. We both needed an escape from work," he said.

"I think we found it," said Rachel, wiping a strand of hair from her forehead.

The ribs came, along with corn on the cob, baked beans and garlic toast. Both were hungry, and both proved enthusiastic eaters.

"The food's great," said Connor.

"And so is the company," added Rachel.

"I hope you'll feel the same way Sunday when we go hiking in the woods by the quarry," observed Connor.

"I'm looking forward to it. Nothing like a hike on a spring day."

"Particularly when you are trying to solve a mystery," he said with a grin.

"I'm always up for a mystery," she responded with a gleam in her eyes.

They finished eating. Connor and Rachel both took out their credit cards, but Connor quickly grabbed the bill on the table. "It's my treat," he told her.

"That's nice of you, but I can pay for my own."

"You can, but not tonight. I've got this one," he said, handing his credit card and the bill to the waitress.

"Thanks, Connor," she said. "One of these days I will treat you to dinner."

"I look forward to it."

When the bill had been paid, Connor and Rachel walked out into the cool spring air. Although the concert and dinner were only blocks from the newspaper office, Connor had driven his SUV.

They both climbed into his Ford Escape and he drove back to the newspaper office to let her off at her car.

He pulled up to her Mini Cooper and shifted his vehicle into park. "I had a great time," Connor told her and leaned over to kiss her on the cheek. She suddenly turned her head toward him, their lips meeting. He kissed her and she responded invitingly, her lips soft and warm.

Just as quickly, they both pulled away. "See you Sunday," said Rachel hurriedly exiting the vehicle. She turned to face him before closing the door. "I enjoyed it," she said.

"Which part?" he asked.

"All of it," she remarked, blowing him a kiss.

CHAPTER TWENTY-NINE

Sunday dawned clear and bright. A lovely spring day. Perfect for a hike in the woods, thought Connor, parking his SUV in the newspaper's parking lot. Rachel showed up a few minutes later in her bright red Mini Cooper. She had the top down. She was wearing black jeans, a blue V-necked T-shirt and black hiking boots. She'd thrown a jacket in the back seat. Her hair was pulled back in a ponytail.

"Climb in," she told Connor, who marveled to himself over how good she looked. Connor wore blue jeans, a brown sweatshirt and hiking boots. Although it was early May, the bugs were beginning to appear. Connor hated bugs, particularly mosquitoes who viewed him as an all-you-can-eat buffet. He brought along a can of OFF to ward off the blood suckers.

"You ready for some hiking and snooping?" he asked.

"You bet. Hopefully, we'll be successful."

"If nothing else, it's a great day for a walk in the woods," said Connor.

"I brought along a picnic basket. I made ham and cheese sandwiches. There's chips too and a thermos of iced tea, plus a few water bottles. Nothing special, but no need to starve."

"Sounds great to me," said Connor, who had considered bringing food, but figured buying some store-bought meals might seem a little lame. And Connor was no cook. The refrigerator in his apartment was largely devoid of any real food. Mostly it served as a beer cooler. He typically ordered out for meals.

Rachel drove across town. She parked her car in the back parking lot of a dentist's office, which bordered the woods. At Connor's suggestion, she put on her jacket to avoid getting scratched by shrub and tree branches. They each brought along a bottle of water.

They walked into the woods, headed toward the edge of the quarry property. The woods were alive with spring. Birds carried on an incessant conversation up in the trees. Squirrels scurried through the undergrowth.

They walked single file, their boots crunching the dead leaves on the forest ground and pushing down the green plants poking up through the soil. Bright green leaves had popped out on the elms, oaks and sweet gums. A few pine trees, reaching high into the sky, staked their claims to the forest too.

A 30-minute hike brought them to the edge of the quarry, which was protected by a tall fence topped with razor wire.

"There's got to be a way around it," said Connor. "No one climbed this fence carrying 50 pounds of dynamite."

"Maybe Tanner or whoever cut a hole in the fence."

"I don't think so. When I talked to Adam, he said the fence was equipped with sensors. There was no evidence of anyone cutting through the fence."

"So, what's the answer?"

"I don't know. Maybe there's a physical feature that aided the theft."

"You mean like a tall boulder?" she asked.

"Something like that," Connor said as he and Rachel walked beside the fence, looking for anything that might offer a way into the quarry.

Forty minutes later, they found it. A portion of the fence was located along the top of three massive boulders. Two of the boulders were wedged atop the lower boulder, leaving a small opening between the rocks.

Connor crawled through the rocky hole, praying he wouldn't come across a snake. The fit was tight, but with a little effort he managed to wrestle his way through the 20-foot-long opening. He stepped out onto a bush-covered, rocky ledge, which stood about four feet above the sloping ground.

Connor heard movement behind him. Rachel had followed him. There was little room on the ledge, forcing Rachel to move her torso next to his.

"That's how the dynamite was removed," said Connor.

"It's definitely possible."

While the quarry was closed on Sunday, Connor and Rachel didn't want to linger. If security guards at the quarry found them, they'd be in serious trouble. They quickly scurried back through the tunnel-like opening. They hiked back the way they came. They made one wrong turn, which took them through a muddy, low spot, forcing them to jump across a narrow creek and climb up the creek bank. It added another 20 minutes to the hike, but other than muddy boots they were no worse for the wear.

They reached Rachel's car, took off their boots and put them in the trunk before putting on tennis shoes they each had brought with them. "You up for a picnic?" she asked, her smiling face radiant in Connor's eyes.

"Sure. But can we find a more scenic spot?"

"I know just the place."

Rachel drove to Elmwood City Park. She steered her Mini Cooper into a parking spot under a shade tree. She climbed out. Connor joined her, taking the picnic basket from the back seat. They walked through the grass, past the city's iconic pond full of geese and ducks and climbed a hill. They found a park bench under an oak tree. Seated, Rachel took out the sandwiches and chips. Connor poured the sweet tea into two red, plastic cups and handed one to Rachel. His cup contained much less of the beverage. He hated sweet tea, but he wasn't going to complain, not today. Rachel was nice enough to bring the picnic lunch. He didn't want to be rude. He'd drink the tea.

They quietly ate their lunch as they watched families stroll through the park and children play on the swings. Couples, holding hands, walked on the trail around the pond. The spring sun had warmed the day. Connor's cell phone showed a temperature of 70, the highest it had been this season. Rachel had ditched her jacket after the hike.

The picnic basket rested on the bench between them, but both felt like they were sitting side by side. There was a closeness about their relationship. They knew it, yet neither wanted to talk about it for fear the feeling would dissipate like a cloud of steam.

After a time, Connor spoke up. "Rachel, I love spending time with you."

"I know. I feel the same way," she said turning to look into his dark eyes. "I don't know where this is going, but let's just take this slow."

"I agree. Any relationship can be tough for co-workers."

"I don't even know that we are in a relationship," replied Rachel. "I don't want to think about it that way. I just want to enjoy whatever it is that we have."

"Me too," said Connor, casting a loving look at her. "Me too."

CHAPTER THIRTY

The man watched the sun rise, painting the sky a bright orange and draping the river in bright, sparkling hues. Clad in jeans and a brown T-shirt, he stood at the edge of the city park overlooking Elmwood's downtown. Morning was breaking this first Saturday of May.

From a distance, the swollen Mississippi seemed ready to reach the top of the floodwall. A dog barked in the distance. The man looked around and saw no one. Downtown was quiet. Those who lived near the riverfront, above the downtown's myriad bars and restaurants, were still asleep and probably hung over from a night of partying or at least listening to the drunks that found it a challenge to navigate the sidewalks after the bars closed.

For now, things were peaceful, like a Currier & Ives print. It could have lasted forever if it weren't for the carefully piled explosives along the riverfront.

The dynamite exploded with a deafening boom, tearing through the vertical seam of the floodgate and the concrete wall. The Mississippi River rushed through the jagged gap, a failing frame of steel and concrete.

Sirens soon sounded throughout the city. Police, fire and emergency personnel rushed to the scene. A young man looked out his downtown loft apartment to see rising, muddy water, turning downtown into a raging river. The man in the park was amazed how quickly the public showed up at a disaster, not really to help, but to gawk at the sight like theatergoers at a horror flick. They wanted to scream. It felt good.

The mayor showed up. Elroy stood and stared at the catastrophe. For once in his life, he was speechless. All the city leaders congregated as close to the disaster as they safely could, including the police chief. Elroy glared at the chief. If looks could kill, the police chief would be dead. Elroy, no doubt, wished Blair Bonney would drown in the raging water.

The police chief, for his part, ignored the criminally charged mayor. Blair knew Elroy would be useless dealing with a disaster of this magnitude.

Teary-eyed Elmwood Chamber of Commerce officials and downtown merchants watched the unfolding disaster, uncertain how to proceed. There were plenty of questions. Did a bomb go off? Did the wall have a structural failure?

Business owners, who had spent years building successful riverfront businesses, wondered if their commercial operations could survive the devastation. Most were already on their cell phones, calling their insurance agents to see if they were sufficiently covered for such a disaster.

Police cordoned off block after block to keep people out of harm's way. A fire truck stalled in the rising water as firefighters tried to reach those trapped in downtown apartments Everywhere one looked, there was chaos, particularly for those who lived and worked downtown.

The man in the park saw people gathered on roofs of buildings, waiting to be rescued. The city's fire/rescue boat was launched into the floodwaters as firefighters worked to rescue those trapped by the deluge. And the water kept coming and coming and coming. At some point, a Missouri Highway Patrol helicopter arrived overhead. A trooper was lowered on a rope to reach about a dozen people stranded on a roof. One by one, they were winched up to the helicopter.

The rescue missions lasted for hours and hours.

By then, the river had turned Elmwood's downtown into a lake, filled with fish, tree limbs and other debris. Parked cars were submerged in the murky water. Downtown businesses were flooded. Dogs could be seen trying to swim to high ground. Cats sought safety in the branches of trees that bordered downtown sidewalks.

Elmwood residents showed up on the river bridge to get a good look at the terrible tragedy. Many were recording the disaster on their cell phones. Missouri's governor had been called. The National Guard would be activated. An engineering battalion would be sent in to try to close the gaping hole. But the man in the park saw such efforts as futile.

Mother Nature was much more powerful than man. She would

crush their miniscule efforts. Elmwood folks had turned their backs on the river. They would regret it, thought the man.

Across the swollen river in East Elmwood, the water was going down. Water was filling up Elmwood's downtown, essentially draining the high water from the Illinois side. East Elmwood residents cheered at the explosion. Soon the strip club would be back in business, providing the kind of entertainment preachers fear.

East Elmwood would survive and thrive. No more would residents there have to live in fear of the wall. The man in the park had seen to that. He embraced the chaos, drinking in the catastrophe. His heart pounding, he took it all in. The news media was there too, television videographers and newspaper photographers captured the destruction, image after image. Connor and Rachel watched in horror.

Emergency personnel set up a staging area in the park. But there was little they could do except watch the watery destruction.

Still, the man stayed, not wanting to leave. He was mesmerized. The outcome was even better than he had hoped for.

No one saw the man. He was as invisible as a ghost. He liked it that way. He grinned at the tragedy taking place. It was better than any horror movie he'd ever seen. But even horror movies had to end.

Regretting he couldn't stay longer, he walked away. Not once did he look back. Seconds later, he awoke in his own bed, covered in sweat. He sat up and wiped his brow. It was just a dream. It was one he had dreamt before, many times. More and more, it seemed real. Soon, he thought, it would be real. He knew it. D-Day was coming. Nothing could stop him; he was sure of it. He would slay that monster wall once and for all.

With that thought in mind, he got out of bed. Time for a shower. No time for dreaming. He had work to do.

CHAPTER THIRTY-ONE

Connor sat a table just inside the front door in Smooth Buns waiting for Rush Johnson to show up. The high-priced defense attorney was late. The meeting had been scheduled for 9 a.m. Rush showed up 20 minutes late, hurrying inside the River Street eatery, having just parked his Tesla in an angled-parking spot.

"Sorry I'm late," he said, greeting Connor. As usual, Rush was dressed to the nines. He was wearing a tan Italian suit, light blue shirt and bowtie and Italian leather dress shoes. On his wrist, he sported a gold Rolex watch. Rush had called Connor, wanting to meet. He figured it had something to do with Elroy's defense, but Rush had not enlightened him during the phone call. Connor and Rush both ordered omelets. Connor had unsweet tea. Rush ordered coffee, black – no sugar or cream.

"So, what's going on?" Connor asked after the waiter departed with their orders."

"One of your co-workers suggested I should speak to you," said Rush.

"Who?"

"Ms. Short," he said to Connor's surprise. "I ran into her at the farmers market. She said you might have information helpful to Elroy."

Connor was silent for a minute. While he personally didn't think Elroy killed Billy, he wanted to cover the story, not become part of the story. "I'm not sure what you want."

"Do you think Elroy shot Billy?" Rush asked bluntly.

"Well, no."

"Then help me. I'll keep your name out of it. What do you know that could aid Elroy's defense?"

Connor gradually told Rush about the can of red paint found in Harvey Winston's office and the red paint dumped on Tanner's vehicle. He talked about the theft of the dynamite, recounted the hike through the woods and finding a way into the fenced-in quarry.

He revealed the friendship Harvey and Tanner had with flood victim Hamilton Jones.

"So, you think either Tanner or Harvey killed Billy?" Rush asked.

"It's possible. Billy saw someone walking in the opposite direction of the floodwall, around 3 a.m., hours before the threatening message was found on the wall."

"That's an interesting theory," observed Rush as the waiter brought them their food.

"That's all it is right now. I can't prove it one way or another," said Connor after the waiter left.

"You don't have to, and I don't either. I just need to show reasonable doubt, and this information could help."

The two men ate their omelets. Both were in a hurry to leave. Rush had to meet a client for a court appearance and Connor had another story to write about the seemingly never-ending flood. Rush downed the rest of his cup of coffee and wiped his mouth with a napkin.

"Thanks, Connor," he said as he stood up and left cash on the table to pay for his meal. "Oh, and you might want to attend Elroy's preliminary hearing. It could prove real interesting."

"I wouldn't miss it," replied Connor as Rush headed out the door. As Conner readied to pay his bill and leave, Oliver sat down at the table. As usual, he was wearing an old sweatshirt, jeans and tennis shoes. The sweatshirt was wine colored and sported an Elmwood College logo. His attire was in clear contrast to that of Rush. Connor, who was wearing jeans himself but paired with a nice dress shirt, felt like he had landed in some sort of fashion feud.

"You looked deep in thought," said Oliver. "I didn't want to interrupt your discussion with Rush."

"We were just talking about Elroy's case."

"I figured that. Anything new?"

"Nothing concrete."

"But you don't believe Elroy killed his nephew, do you?"

"No, but I'm not sure who did. Whoever did it planted the murder weapon in the mayor's office?"

"Any ideas?"

"Maybe."

"Maybe what? Spill it. Don't keep secrets from your favorite restauranteur."

"Well, there are two possible suspects," he began, identifying Tanner and Harvey, and briefly recounting his investigation. "Now, don't go spreading it around," cautioned Connor.

"Don't worry. Who would I tell, except Truman."

"Well, he's as talkative as you are. So, that's not much consolation," said Connor.

"I promise we won't go blabbing it about. Besides, as you say, there are a lot of questions, but few answers in this murder case. We surely don't want to get sued."

"I don't either," replied Connor. "But I feel I'm close to solving it."

"Well, I hope you solve it before someone blows up the floodwall and washes out my beautiful business."

"I hope so too," said Connor. "I'd hate to see Smooth Buns destroyed. Where would I eat breakfast?"

"Exactly," said Oliver. "And we both know how you like your breakfast." They both laughed. Connor paid his bill and 15 minutes later was back in the newsroom.

He walked over to Rachel who had just finished a phone call with the local school superintendent. "Why didn't you tell me about your conversation with Rush?"

"I just ran into him. It wasn't planned, Connor."

"Yeah, he told me. I just had a lengthy discussion with Rush. So why did you suggest he talk to me?"

"I thought if Rush knew some of the things we knew, he might be able to raise those issues in defending Elroy."

"And?"

"And if Rush starts making statements, it might bring the killer out into the open. He might make a mistake that would lead to his arrest. If an attorney raises some of these issues, maybe the police would look to really solve this case instead of trying to pin it on Elroy."

"Well, I wish you had talked to me first."

"And if I had? You would have instructed me not to talk to Rush."

"Yes, probably so," said Connor.

"But do you see my point, how it might help us catch a killer?"

"I do, although I'm not sure Bare Bones wants to really solve this case. He and Elroy aren't exactly friends. But from now on, talk to me first. I don't want to be blindsided. And you've got to be careful around Rush. He will do anything to defend his clients, even if it means throwing us under the bus."

"I promise. No more loose lips at the farmers market."

"Or anywhere else," said Connor.

"Or anywhere else," agreed Rachel, directing a soft smile in his direction.

CHAPTER THIRTY-TWO

The courtroom was packed. Family, friends and political supporters of Mayor Elroy James filled the place for his preliminary hearing on the murder charge. Some even sported buttons proclaiming, "Free the Mayor."

Seated on the bench in his black robe, Judge Donald Fisher eyed the crowd. This wasn't a normal preliminary hearing. That was obvious from the crowd that had gathered, including a number of reporters who seldom ever covered such preliminary legal proceedings.

In most criminal cases, preliminary hearings were nothing more than a formality. Most defendants were poor and represented by overworked public defenders who regularly convinced their clients to waive the hearings.

But that wouldn't be the case this time. The mayor wasn't represented by a public defender. He was represented by Elmwood's most able and high-priced attorney, Rush Johnson. As usual, Rush was dressed in the best blue suit money could buy. He wore a blue shirt with white pinstripes and a white bowtie. He wore fine leather, black dress shoes.

The prosecutor, Richard Lamb, on the other hand, sported a black department store suit, light blue Oxford shirt in need of ironing, navy blue tie and black dress shoes from the discount shoe store in Elmwood.

Connor had a front row seat to the courtroom drama.

Judge Fisher pounded his gavel, bringing the hearing to order. "Before we begin, I want to advise those in the audience to refrain from making any comments during this proceeding. Anyone who disrupts this hearing will be escorted from the courtroom by the bailiff and will not be allowed back in."

With that, Lamb called his first and, not surprisingly for a preliminary hearing, only witness, police detective Adam Dade.

After establishing Adam's experience in law enforcement, the prosecutor asked the detective about the stolen dynamite and the shooting death of Billy Moss.

"As I understand it, he was shot at close range behind the Alligator Alley restaurant?"

"Yes, two shots into the head."

"What type of weapon was used?"

"A Colt 1911 style semi-automatic pistol."

"Why did Mr. James threaten Billy?"

"He told police that he knew Billy had distributed those Bible verses about flooding and was concerned his nephew may have written the threatening message on the floodwall."

"And did you find the murder weapon?"

"Yes, I found it in a search of Elroy's office at city hall."

"How do you know it was the murder weapon?"

"Ballistic tests proved it was the gun used in the shooting," Adam said.

When Lamb finished his questioning, Rush got up to cross examine the detective.

"Mr. Dade, were you surprised to find the murder weapon in the mayor's office?"

"Yes."

"Why is that?"

"He didn't strike me as a murderer, him being mayor and all."

"Was the gun hidden in Elroy's office?" Rush asked, standing close to Adam, who was seated in the witness chair.

"It was buried under a stack of legal pads in a bottom drawer of his desk."

"Not very hidden, in my mind," observed Rush, looking at the mayor's supporters. "Do you think that would be a good place for the mayor to hide a murder weapon?"

"I don't know what the mayor thinks. It wasn't that hard for me to find. So, I guess you could say it wasn't a great hiding place."

"If Elroy shot Billy, don't you think he would have ditched the gun somewhere else, not in his city hall office?"

"Like I said, I don't know what Elroy might have thought at the time."

"Yeah. Well, I don't think it makes much sense for Elroy to hide the gun in his office. It only makes sense if the mayor was framed by the actual murderer," Rush observed.

"Objection, your honor," said Lamb, popping up from his chair. "There's no evidence that Mr. James was framed or that anyone else did the shooting."

"Judge, the defense's position is that the mayor didn't shoot his nephew. The defense has every right to pursue this line of questioning."

"I will allow it," Fisher ruled. "Objection overruled."

Lamb collapsed back into his chair, clearly unhappy with the ruling.

"When you questioned Mr. James, what did he say about the gun?" asked Rush.

"He said it wasn't his."

"In fact, Mr. Dade, didn't the mayor tell police he never owned a handgun?"

"Yes, he did."

After Adam finished testifying, Rush told the judge he planned to call two defense witnesses. Judge Fisher looked surprised.

He beckoned the prosecutor and defense attorney to the bench for a private discussion.

"What are you doing, Rush?" the judge asked.

"Presenting my case," he replied.

"Yes, but you realize this is a preliminary hearing. The prosecution only has to show minimal evidence that your client might have committed murder. That's not a high bar."

"Yes, I realize that, Judge. But Elroy is not just any defendant. He is a beloved public figure and as such his reputation is begin attacked. He needs to defend himself even at this stage of the proceedings, and I intend to present his case at every step."

Lamb started to object, but Fisher waved him to be quiet. "If the defense wants to present witnesses at this hearing, go ahead."

With that, the hearing continued. To Connor's surprise, Rush called Tanner Holloway to the stand.

Tanner was wearing a brown sportscoat and collared shirt which was accented with a "Save the Planet" tie. He was sworn in to "tell the truth" and took the witness seat.

In rapid fire, Rush asked Tanner about his career as an environmental science professor and his belief that dams and levees make flooding worse.

"You have written in a newspaper opinion piece that Mississippi River flooding would be lessened if floodwalls like Elmwood's were removed. Is that correct?"

"Yes, that's true."

"So, you would have a reason to want to blow up the wall, maybe with the stolen dynamite?"

"I'm not a murderer," said Tanner. "You're trying to paint me as some sort of terrorist."

"Didn't you once work at the quarry?"

"While I was in college, yes."

"So, you would have known where the dynamite was stored?"

"Well, yes, but that was a long time ago."

Lamb rose. "Judge, clearly Mr. Johnson is throwing out a ridiculous theory. There is no evidence that Mr. Holloway has been anything, but an outstanding college professor. Besides, the dynamite was stolen fairly recently, not years ago when Mr. Holloway would have worked there."

Judge Fisher nodded his head. "Let's move on," he instructed Rush.

Upon further questioning, Tanner talked about his friendship with flood victim Hamilton Jones.

"Mr. Jones owned a semi-automatic pistol like the one that killed Billy, correct?"

"Yes."

"And you often shot that pistol at competitions?"

"Yes."

"Do you know what happened to that gun after Mr. Jones died in that flood?"

"No, I don't."

"Are you aware if anyone else ever used Mr. Jones' Colt pistol?"

"Yes, Harvey Winston. He was a friend of Hamilton. And he owned handguns too."

Rush wrapped up his questioning of Tanner and then called Harvey to the stand, yet again surprising Connor, who was hurriedly scribbling notes.

East Elmwood's mayor was dressed in a green polo shirt and tan pants and gray tennis shoes. He seemed nervous, Connor thought.

Upon questioning, Harvey said he didn't know how the can of red paint, the color used on the wall graffiti, had ended up in his office in the East Elmwood City Hall, nor how the identical color of red paint ended up on Tanner's vehicle across the river.

He acknowledged he knew Tanner and that both men had been close to flood victim Hamilton Jones. Harvey also disclosed that Tanner was an expert marksman, having won pistol competitions with the same model of handgun used to murder the bartender.

"But isn't it true you also shot Mr. Jones' Colt pistol on occasion?" asked Rush, again peering at Elroy's supporters in the audience.

"Yeah, a few times."

"And at one time you owned a large collection of handguns, including a Colt pistol like Mr. Jones had."

"That's true, I did. But I sold them a while back."

"As mayor of East Elmwood, I believe you have stated that your town's flooding problem would be lessened if Elmwood didn't have a massive floodwall."

"I am sure I have. Everyone in East Elmwood shares that view, but that doesn't mean I stole the dynamite and intended to blow up the wall or murdered Billy."

"Right," Rush said, clearly expressing doubt in his voice.

Again, Lamb countered. "Judge, Mr. Johnson is once again throwing out a theory that has no basis in fact."

The judge ignored the remark and turned his attention to Rush. "Anymore testimony, Mr. Johnson?"

"No, your honor. Other than to say that the testimony of Mr. Holloway and Mr. Winston indicate that both view the floodwall as a problem and seemingly would favor removing it. Both worked at the quarry and knew where the dynamite was stored. Police have reported 50 pounds of dynamite was stolen from the quarry. Both men admit to having fired a semi-automatic pistol like the one determined to have been the murder weapon. Either one could have shot Billy," suggested Johnson.

"So, what was the motive for killing Mr. Moss?" the judge asked.

"Well," said Rush, "it's clear Billy saw someone walking away from the direction of the floodwall and carrying a can of paint in the middle of the night. A threatening message was found painted on the floodwall. Assuming the man with the paint can wrote that message, that person subsequently could have shot Billy out of fear that he could identify him."

"Judge, Mr. Johnson is spouting pure fantasy," Lamb said. "According to police, Mr. Moss could not identify the man carrying the paint can. There's no reason for that individual to shoot Mr. Moss. The only person with a clear motive for shooting Mr. Moss is Elroy James. The state asks that he be bound over for trial."

"Anything else, Mr. Lamb? Anything else, Mr. Johnson?"

"No, your Honor," both attorneys said in unison.

"Very well, I find that there is sufficient evidence for the prosecution to take the case against Elroy James to trial," said Fisher, pounding the gavel to end the proceeding. The judge hurriedly left the bench as an audible sound of disbelief and dismay circulated throughout the audience. But neither Rush nor Elroy seemed concerned.

Elroy walked over to the crowd to shake hands and accept their well wishes. Connor watched the action. It struck him that Elroy acted more like a political campaigner than a criminal defendant. Even facing a murder charge, Elroy played to the crowd, and so had Rush.

The defense attorney knew the outcome of the preliminary hearing before it even started. Rush was playing to the public, Connor knew. And he figured Judge Fisher knew it too.

CHAPTER THIRTY-THREE

Back in the newsroom, Connor put down his notebook filled with scribbled words of what had taken place at the preliminary hearing. "You won't believe what happened," he told Rachel.

"Elroy pleaded guilty," she jokingly remarked.

"No. Tanner and Harvey were both called as defense witnesses. Rush tried to show that either of them had a motive to shoot Billy, which focused on wanting to blow up the floodwall."

"I guess your recent conversation with Rush aided the defense," she said.

"Seems so," replied Connor as Lansmon approached.

"I just heard about the defense witnesses," said Lansmon. "I want to see you both in my office." The three of them convened minutes later around a small conference table in the editor's sparsely decorated office. Lansmon didn't bother hanging a lot of pictures on the wall. He could care less about how his office looked. Besides the enlarged Shoe comics, one wall held a poster reproduction of the Chicago Daily Tribune's famously incorrect "Dewey Defeats Truman" headline. Other than that, the white office walls were bare.

Seated at the table, Lansmon didn't bother with small talk. Rather, he delivered his message like a general issuing marching orders. No debate, no discussion, just orders.

"Today's preliminary hearing has turned Tanner and Harvey into suspects. As a result, we need to take a closer look at them. Find out if defense attorney Rush Johnson's arguments have any merit. We also need to see if the police are now taking a closer look at them, and, if not, why not."

"So, we don't have to treat Tanner with kid gloves anymore?" asked Connor.

"No. That policy went away when Tanner testified. Connor, see what you can find out about Harvey's former gun collection and his prowess with guns, particularly a semi-automatic pistol like the one used to kill Billy Moss."

"You don't want me to check on Tanner?"

"No. You already pissed him off," he told Connor. "Rachel, I want you to drill down on Tanner. See if you can find anything that would tie him to Billy's murder and/or any effort to blow up the wall."

"I'll get right on it," said Rachel. Connor looked at her and saw the spark in her eyes. He knew she was excited about the prospect of possibly tracking down a killer. Her look said it all. She was thrilled to be on the chase. It was also what Connor liked about investigative journalism, the ability to uncover wrongdoing that people sought to cover up.

Within an hour, Connor had managed to reach Harvey on his cellphone. It took a little doing, but he convinced Harvey that it would be in his best interest to be interviewed about his past gun collection. Connor told him it would show that he had nothing to hide.

The two men chose to meet at the Elmwood Mansion. Connor had suggested the location after first checking with museum director Henry Carter. Henry, dressed in his usual spiffy attire, greeted them at the door and showed them to a small conference room located off the mansion's foyer. He wished them both well and left to attend to his museum duties. He never even asked them why they wanted to meet there. It didn't matter to him. The room was available so why not use it, Henry reasoned.

"I can't believe people think I am a murderer," Harvey angrily told Connor. "That damn Rush. He subpoenaed me. I thought he was just going to ask me about Tanner. I didn't know he would try to make me look like the bad guy because of my gun collection."

"He just tried to deflect attention away from the mayor," Connor observed.

"Well, I'm sure he succeeded," Harvey lamented.

"Tell me about your gun collection. I understand you had a number of handguns."

"Yeah. It was kind of a hobby for me. I always liked owning and shooting them. At one time, I probably had about 30 handguns, everything from single-action and double-action revolvers to semi-automatic pistols."

"Did you ever own a Colt 1911?"

"Yeah. I had three of them. I had other semi-automatic pistols too, including a Beretta 92, a number of Glocks and even a Walther PPK like the one made famous in those James Bond movies. I owned a number of revolvers too, including a .357 magnum Smith & Wesson. I loved that gun. It was great to shoot. I had a Colt 45 'Peacemaker' revolver. It was an antique, dated back to the late 1800s. Like I said, I just loved the guns. I loved to hold them. I appreciated their craftsmanship. I used to display them in my house, but I quit doing that after some guns were stolen from a friend of mine. I bought myself a huge gun safe and kept them in there until I sold them."

"Did you keep any guns?"

"Yeah. I still have some rifles. I like to deer hunt."

"But you sold all the handguns?"

"I sold all about four years ago, except for one Glock. I keep that around for protection."

"Why did you sell your collection when it gave you such joy?" asked Connor.

"Well, frankly, I'm getting older. Being mayor takes up a lot of my time. I don't have the time to target practice like I used to. What good is it to have a gun collection stored in a safe where you can't view them? Also, it worried my wife Frannie to have so many guns around. So, I sold the handguns. I made a little money, so that's good too."

Connor steered the conversation back to the Colt 1911. "At the preliminary hearing, you testified that you shot Hamilton's pistol a few times."

"Yes, just for fun. I didn't shoot it in competition like Tanner did."

"But you admit, you at one time owned several Colt 1911 pistols and you liked shooting them at targets."

"Yes, on the property of a farmer friend of mine. My guns were never used in competition. Just because I like shooting guns doesn't make me a murderer."

"And you have no idea what happened to Hamilton's pistol?"

"No clue. Tanner might have inherited it. I don't know. I wasn't part of the family, just friends with Hamilton, not his relatives."

"Harvey, have you thought about blowing up the floodwall?"

"I told you I am not some terrorist. Besides, I am too busy trying to save my town to commit such a crime."

"But you admitted in court that if the wall fails, it would provide flood relief to East Elmwood, take the pressure off your village's earthen levee."

"Yes, but that doesn't mean I am going to blow up the wall. That's crazy," said Harvey, his voice agitated.

"Okay, I'm not saying you want to do that. I am just trying to put myself in your shoes, see the flooding situation from your perspective."

"I'm sorry. This whole thing just has upset me."

"One last thing. Assuming someone was planning to blow up the wall, when would he do it?"

"Soon, I would think," said Harvey. "The flood crest is coming soon."

Connor nodded his head. He thought the same thing. Tick tock, tick tock. If there was a bomber out there, he needed to be found soon or it would be too late. After Harvey departed, Connor headed outside and found a bench on the mansion grounds. He wanted a quiet place to think as storm clouds threatened the sky. Harvey seemed sincerely upset. Maybe he was telling the truth, Connor thought. But how could he be sure? Connor had no answer even as the Mississippi River climbed higher and higher on the wall.

CHAPTER THIRTY-FOUR

Harvey Winston had just left the Elmwood Mansion after being grilled by Connor when his cell phone rang. It was Maj. Gen. Ted Walsh. The Army Corps of Engineers commander sounded tired and uneasy.

"You have a minute? We need to meet. It's urgent," said Walsh.

"I'm on your side of the river right now."

"Great. Come by my office," Walsh said, ending the conversation. The call left Harvey grasping for answers. What did Walsh want?

Eight minutes later, Harvey found a parking spot on River Street and parked his late-model, slightly rusting pickup in front of a former real estate office, which was now home to the Corps' emergency headquarters for the ongoing flood fight. The small space was crowded with engineering staff. Flood maps were spread out on a conference table. Walsh came forward to greet Harvey before ushering him into a small room in the back.

"Thanks for coming," Walsh said as he closed the door. He sat down at his desk and Harvey took a seat across from him.

"So, what's this about?" Harvey said.

"My staff and I have been discussing options on how to protect Elmwood's downtown from flooding if the river keeps rising." Walsh hesitated before speaking again. Harvey noticed the pause with alarm. "We've come to the conclusion that residents in East Elmwood should evacuate."

"Why? We are holding our own," said Harvey.

"Because the Army Corps is considering blowing holes in East Elmwood's agricultural levee to relieve the pressure on the Missouri wall," Walsh replied, his eyes trained tightly on Harvey.

The East Elmwood mayor sank into the chair and let out a huge sigh before regaining his composure and a take-no-prisoners attitude. "You can't do that," he said, "You want to save a rich city at the expense of us poor folks in East Elmwood. That's unfair. You have no right to do that."

"Actually, we have every right. We blew up an earthen levee on the Missouri side some years ago to save Cairo, Illinois. We can do it now on the Illinois side to save Elmwood," Walsh said. "We hope it's not necessary, but East Elmwood residents should evacuate within the next seven days just in case we have to blow the levee."

"You're crazy. The folks in East Elmwood will fight this every way we can. The federal government has no right to wipe out our village."

"Well, the Corps is moving ahead with planning for possible demolition. I will be delivering that message at a news conference within the hour. I just wanted to let you know first."

"Thanks for the consideration," Harvey replied sarcastically. "I'm warning you. Don't mess with my village."

"Is that a threat? Do you plan to blow up the floodwall?" asked Walsh.

"I didn't say that."

"I wouldn't if I were you," said Walsh, staring harshly at Harvey. "That would be a crime."

"Oh, but it's not a crime for the Army Corps of Engineers to blow up levees at will," retorted Harvey.

"Listen, Harvey. Blowing up the East Elmwood levee is an action of last resort. We hope that's not necessary, but the fact of the matter is that there are more people who would be impacted by flooding on the Missouri side than over in Illinois."

"I see it a lot differently. I guess I'll have to hope the floodwall is breached. It would save my town."

"Harvey, you need to think of the greater good."

"I am. On my side of the river, things would be far better if that wall had never been built."

"Well, it's built and it's staying that way," said Walsh.

Harvey rose and headed for the door. "This isn't over," he told Walsh, "not by a long shot."

The news conference occurred downtown, in front of the floodgate. With reporters and cameramen crowded around, Walsh delivered the news, urging East Elmwood residents to evacuate. "I want to encourage all residents of the village to heed this message. Staying could put you in harm's way," he said.

Walsh repeated several times that the Corps hoped demolition would not be necessary. "It all depends on the river," he said before being peppered with reporters' questions.

"Are you preparing for demolition now?" asked a young, blonde TV reporter wearing a bright red skirt and a white, short-sleeved blouse.

"We are. We are loading a barge in Memphis with liquid explosives, which will be transported upriver within the next several days."

When the scrum of reporters had left, Connor approached. "Maj. Gen. Walsh, aren't you concerned that your public announcement might make it more likely that someone would try to blow up the floodwall?"

"No, I'm not concerned. It's not that easy to blow up the wall. It takes planning and it takes some skill to set explosives and detonate them. East Elmwood residents may say they want to blow up the wall, but that's a far cry from actually committing such an act."

Connor nodded, but secretly he wasn't so sure. As he walked away, he spotted Elroy, who was standing a short distance away on the sidewalk. Connor approached the mayor. "How are you doing, Elroy?"

"Okay, I guess, for an innocent man accused of murder," he replied.

"What did you think of the Major General's announcement?"

"Well, it wasn't a surprise. Ted advised me of the news in advance."

"Did you agree with it?"

"You mean the idea of demolishing the Illinois levee if necessary?"

"Yeah."

"I agree with it. I don't want to see East Elmwood destroyed, but I think it would be worse to allow the flood to demolish our downtown. Either way, it's a terrible situation. But I believe it's important to preserve our downtown at all costs."

"Even if it means the possible destruction of East Elmwood?" asked Connor.

"Yes, even then," replied Elroy. "But I hope it doesn't come to that."

"I hope so too," said Connor. "And I hope no one blows up the floodwall."

"Me too," said Elroy. "And Connor, you know one thing for sure. If someone does try to destroy the wall, it won't be me."

Connor didn't reply but, in his mind, he agreed. Elroy wasn't a bomber. Besides, the mayor loved the floodwall almost as much as those ugly sculptures around town, Connor thought.

But someone wanted to destroy the wall, Connor believed. In light of the major general's announcement, would Harvey try to blow up the wall? Or what about Tanner? Maybe, thought Connor, it's all about a family tragedy, blood and water.

CHAPTER THIRTY-FIVE

Rachel left work early. She had finished a feature story on how students in poverty were struggling academically, navigating a minefield of family trauma at home and the inability to concentrate in the classroom.

She decided to browse her favorite downtown antique store. Housed in a former grocery store, "This & That" offered everything from old china dishes and vintage furniture to antique toys and old books and magazines. Betsy Bertrand operated the shop. Her cash register sat atop an old, wooden workbench at the front of the store. Betsy, who was in her 70s, greeted everyone who walked through the door. Most, like Rachel, were repeat customers whom she knew by name.

Rachel was greeted immediately by Betsy when she opened the door to the shop. Rachel smiled at the shopkeeper. "How are you doing, Betsy?"

"Just fine, Rachel. You ready to part with some of your money? There's an antique typewriter you might like."

"You know me too well," Rachel laughingly replied. "I just thought I'd look around. Maybe get some inspiration to redo my apartment."

"Honey, that's what my shop offers. Lots of inspiration," Betsy said, a broad grin sweeping across her face.

"That's why I'm here," agreed Rachel.

She spent the next half hour wandering through the aisles crowded with all manner of antiques. She gazed at vintage dolls, radios and kitchenware. An old, wooden icebox drew her attention, as did a black, 1922 Remington typewriter. She loved vintage type-writers. Her collection now numbered seven. Her most cherished was a Blickensderfer No. 6 typewriter, manufactured in 1911. Rachel spied an "alligator red" 1930s Royal P typewriter on a wooden shelf next to an antique bowling pen. She thought of buying it but decided she didn't want to pay the $210 price, at least not yet.

She still hadn't been down every aisle. She might find something else. One aisle over, she did. Resting on the arms of a vintage wicker chair, Rachel spotted a wood-framed watercolor. The painting seemed out of place. It didn't look terribly old. But the image, created in bold colors, startled her. It was a large piece, 36 by 48 inches. It depicted a flooded river breaking through a downtown floodwall and swamping stores and homes. Townsfolk depicted in the scene wore anguished looks. Some clearly were drowning. Others were clinging to balconies. The painter portrayed the flooding with bold slashes of color, ranging from greenish brown and dull yellow to dark blue and black. She looked for the painter's name in the corner of the picture but found none.

Intrigued, she hurriedly walked to the front of the store. "Do you know anything about that flood painting?" she asked Betsy.

"Interesting isn't it?"

"Definitely. But it doesn't seem that old."

"I agree. I only took it because it came with a bunch of items I purchased from an old estate. I found it taped to the underside of an old dining room table, almost like someone was ashamed of it. Strange, to say the least."

"Sure is. Do you know who painted it?"

"No, but you might ask Lou Lucas."

"The guy who paints murals?"

"Yeah, he knows just about every artist in town. If the guy is local, he would know," said Betsy.

"Good idea. And I'll take the painting," Rachel replied.

Betsy walked to the back of the store to retrieve the painting. She returned to the workbench where she quickly and neatly wrapped the work of art in brown paper and taped the ends.

Rachel paid for the painting with cash after getting Betsy to lower the price from $300, which she thought was ridiculously high, to $150. She carried it out to her red Mini Cooper and placed it on its side behind the front seats. She needed to see Lou. Hopefully, he could tell her who painted it. There was a story behind the painting. She wanted to know it.

***

Two hours later, the tall man sat on his dark leather couch replaying the 5 p.m. news he had taped. He could care less about the 15 minutes of weather. His focus was on the top story: The Corps of Engineers' plan to blow up the East Elmwood levee, if necessary, to save downtown Elmwood.

The news made him sick to his stomach and angry. He was so mad, he wanted to scream. On his large-screen TV he watched Maj. Gen. Walsh's announcement over and over again. That pompous ass, dressed in his stiffly starched military uniform, was calmly explaining why the village of East Elmwood was expendable. Watching the news, the man wanted to strangle Walsh or, better yet, drown him. Drown him in the muddy Mississippi. That would serve him right. What Walsh had said was tantamount to a death sentence for the Illinois village. The man on the couch was certain of that. And, he was just as certain he could stop it and save the town. All he had to do was blow up the floodwall. There would be no need to blow up the agricultural level protecting East Elmwood. He had to finish making plans for the demolition. Dynamiting the wall would lead to the flooding of Elmwood's downtown, but the rich merchants could rebuild. They had money. What did people in East Elmwood have? Almost nothing. Many of them lived on Social Security and food stamps, the man told himself. His plan was righteous. Walsh's was evil, he believed.

The man had to act, and soon. He was running out of time. Walsh's statement made it clear. Bold action was coming. Soon, the news media would have a stunning story to tell of his heroic action. People would see him as a savior, not just someone seeking revenge. He liked that narrative. He smiled at the thought of being a hero. East Elmwood residents were counting on him. He wouldn't let them down. Not now, not when he was so close to achieving his goal.

The man rose from the couch and walked into the kitchen. He took a $50 bottle of Rombauer chardonnay out of the fridge, uncorked it, and poured himself a glass of the smooth white wine. Then he returned to the living room ready to rerun the awful news again, the image of Ted Walsh scorched into his mind like a horrible "Halloween" movie nightmare.

CHAPTER THIRTY-SIX

Lou's place was deserted, a day after Rachel purchased the flood painting. She showed up at his place around 10 a.m. on a day when billowing white clouds played hide and seek with the sun.

Lou lived in a two-story, square, brick building three blocks from the floodwall. Built in the early 1900s, it once housed a popular tavern on the first floor. Lou bought the building in the early 2000s. He lived upstairs. He turned the first floor into a gallery to display and sell his artwork. Rachel repeatedly rang the doorbell. No answer. The lights were off in the gallery. She peered through the large, display windows, searching for any sign of Lou. He wasn't there. Rachel figured he was probably out painting some mural or romancing some woman. At age 38 and single, Lou was a notorious womanizer. Maybe that could work to her advantage, she reasoned.

Rachel decided to drive around the historic downtown. Lou had painted numerous murals on brick buildings along Main and River streets. Maybe he was painting another one. She drove around the downtown, turning on every side street and looking down every alley. After about 15 minutes, she found him high up on a scaffold, painting an image of a nude woman on the side of a brick building which housed the Jello night club.

She parked her Mini Cooper next to the curb and climbed out. Lou, dressed in jeans and a St. Louis Cardinals T-shirt, both covered in paint stains, was carefully painting the woman's left breast in various hues of white.

Rachel called out. "I see you are working on another mural," she told Lou. He looked down from atop the scaffold.

"Oh, hi Rachel. Haven't seen you since you did that feature piece on me about a year ago."

"Yeah. Well, I've been around. You're just too focused on your work to notice," she said with a laugh.

"Probably right," replied Lou, who wore his long, brown hair in a ponytail.

"Do you have time to come down and talk? I need to show you something."

"Sure. I can take a break. I'll be right down."

Lou carefully put down his brush and descended the scaffold with practiced ease. He reached the last rung on the scaffold and stepped onto the sidewalk.

"So, what do you want to show me?" he asked.

"I bought a painting that intrigues me."

"You didn't buy one of mine," he said with a pretend pout.

"No, I got this at the antique store," she admitted. Rachel carefully unwrapped the painting she had placed behind the car seats. She lifted it up and handed it to him. Lou eyed the painting, looking at the bold colors and brush strokes. He peered closely at the bottom right corner and then nodded his head.

"It's a Win," he said confidently. "You can see the signature."

"Where? I didn't see a signature."

"It's really small. See those lines at the end of that black swash near the bottom of the painting." Rachel looked closely at the lines as Lou reached his arm over her shoulder pointing to the spot. There were tiny short brush strokes spelling the letters WIN.

"Win? What kind of name is that?" she asked.

"The name of a gifted painter," he replied.

"Is the painter a he or a she?"

"I believe it's a man. I have never met him, but I have seen his paintings. The local arts council displayed some of the paintings several years ago. Dr. Holloway loaned the paintings for the exhibit."

"Tanner Holloway?"

"Yeah, that's the guy. He owns about a dozen Win paintings."

"Do all those paintings deal with floods?"

"Yes, as a matter of fact, they do. Kind of strange if you ask me, but they definitely are unique. There's raw emotion expressed in those images. They make you feel like you are drowning."

"They do," agreed Rachel.

"Did Tanner tell you anything about the artist."

"He didn't say much. I got the impression Win isn't the painter's real name. Dr. Holloway was very guarded about the painter's identity. For all I know, Dr. Holloway could have been the painter.

He seemed obsessed with the paintings."

"Thanks for the information," said Rachel as she placed the painting back in her car and covered it again in the brown paper, taping the ends as best she could.

"Well, I got to get back to my girl," Lou said, pointing to the nude on the wall. "But stop by any time, Rachel. I'd love to hang out with you."

"I'm sure you would," she smilingly observed. "Some people think you're a Casanova."

"I do my best," he yelled down to her as he deftly climbed up the scaffold. He briefly turned his body back toward her and blew her a kiss. Rachel waved off the attention and climbed into her car. She needed to find Tanner and uncover the origins of those paintings. What was he hiding? Who really painted those flood scenes? She hoped Tanner would talk to her. So far, he hadn't returned any of her calls or emails wanting to interview him and get his reaction to the defense attorney's suggestion that he may have murdered Billy. She had to find a way to gain his confidence so he would open up to her. The paintings, she reasoned, might be just the ticket to getting Tanner to sit down with her. She'd get him to talk about those paintings. Maybe such conversation would open a window into his soul, give her a glimpse of what truly made him angry. It just might provide a clue as to whether Tanner Holloway was a murderer, Rachel thought.

The more she considered it, the more she was certain she had to find a way to get into Tanner's house. He was clearly guarded at the college. In his home, he might be more at ease. He might let his guard down, she told herself, particularly since she now owned a Win painting.

CHAPTER THIRTY-SEVEN

Connor was amazed. Flood paintings. And they were tied in some way to Tanner Holloway. Rachel's journey into the art world might hold the key to unlocking this mystery, Connor thought as his coworker recounted her conversation with Lou Lucas.

Rachel had carried the painting into the newsroom and placed it on her desk. Connor eyed the bold slashes of color. The artist's technique conveyed a sense of raging mayhem. Clearly, the flood was personal to this painter.

Lansmon strolled out of his office to see the painting for himself. "Not Monet," he observed. "But it's intriguing to say the least. Are you planning to hang it in your apartment?"

"Yeah. But right now, I hope to use it as bait to get Tanner to open up to me," Rachel said, once again detailing her discussion with Lou.

"Good idea," agreed Lansmon. "Just one thing, don't even try to get the paper to reimburse you for the cost of that artwork."

"Don't worry. Your budget is safe," Rachel replied.

"Well, then carry on," Lansmon said, retreating to his office.

"So, how are you going to approach Tanner?" Connor asked after Lansmon had left.

"I initially thought about just walking into his faculty office with the painting."

"Might be too bold," responded Connor, who had rolled his chair next to her desk and taken a seat. "He may be uneasy about talking at work where fellow faculty members or students might be intrigued by the painting."

"I was thinking the same thing. It might be best to just show up at his house."

"You could. But I've got a better idea. Why not take a photo of you painting on your cell phone and email it to him?"

Rachel agreed. She took a photo of the painting, which she had placed on her desk. Then with a press of an icon, she sent the painting to Tanner as an attachment. The message read: "Tanner, love the artwork. Now I own a Win painting. Can we talk?"

Hours went by, no reply, Rachel was beginning to despair of ever getting Tanner to talk to her. Then shortly after lunch, her cell phone pinged. She had an email. She opened it and read the message. "Congratulations, you should be honored to own such a painting. I'd love to see it. Can you bring it over to my house, say 7 p.m.?"

Rachel quickly replied, "Yes, that's great."

She turned to Connor. "He's agreed to meet me at his house. Hopefully, Tanner will show me his Win paintings, and then maybe I can discover who the artist is."

"Be careful, Rachel. Tanner's not going to crack easily. And, if he is a murderer, he could murder again if he feels threatened."

"Why Connor, are you worried about me? How nice," she told him, her eyes sparkling with delight.

"I'm serious," said Connor. "If you feel uncomfortable, end the conversation and leave."

"I'll be fine. If Tanner was going to murder a reporter, it would be you," she replied.

"You're probably right," agreed Connor with a laugh.

Rachel showed up at Tanner's house promptly at 7 p.m. She was dressed in tight blue jeans, a frilly white blouse and black dress sandals. She pressed the brass doorbell and heard the ding-dong sound floating through the home.

She heard brisk footsteps. Tanner opened the door. He was dressed in gray jeans and his favorite "Save the Planet" T-shirt and scuffed tennis shoes.

"Glad you came," he said. She was holding the brown-paper-wrapped painting. He took it from her and led her into the dining room. He placed the item on the table and carefully unwrapped it. His eyes glistened with excitement. Clearly, she saw, Tanner wanted to see this painting.

After unwrapping it, he stared for several minutes at it, not saying a word. Finally, he let out a sigh. "Wow. Isn't it beautiful? I had no idea there was another Win painting."

"I'm not sure I would say it's beautiful, maybe eerie is a better description," she said.

"No, you're mistaken. It is truly beautiful, a real work of art.

144

Look at those brush strokes. They are pure genius." Tanner motioned for Rachel to take a seat at the table. She did and then he sat down across the table from her.

"So, how did you obtain this painting?" he asked.

"I found it at an antique store, "This & That," replied Rachel.

"Betsy's place," he said, nodding. "I've bought a few pieces of vintage furniture from her, including an old, wooden icebox. I just liked the look of it."

"Yeah, it's a great place. I love to browse."

"How much did you pay for it, if I can ask?"

"I paid $150 cash," she proudly replied.

"That's a steal," he said. "I would have paid double that price."

Rachel smiled, the look telling him she knew she got a good deal. "Lou Lucas told me that you have a number of Win paintings yourself."

"Yes. I have a dozen such paintings."

"Do they all deal with flooding?"

"Yes. It's a series. The scenes are slightly different, but they all deal with flooding. They are all numbered on the back. I had no idea there were 13. You want to see the paintings?" he asked.

"Sure. I'd love to," replied Rachel. Tanner rose and headed through a door leading from the dining room into a hallway. She followed. He led her down the wood-floored hallway before turning into a large, open room. Rachel thought it probably once had been a bedroom. Now, it was an art gallery of sorts. No furniture graced the room. But the white, plastered walls were decorated with the flood paintings. They were placed evenly around the room. The effect was mesmerizing. She stood and stared at the swooshes of bright, dark colors that covered each canvas. Each piece was framed the same, with carved mahogany that seemed to draw even more attention to the collection.

Most of the paintings showed drowning downtown scenes. But one stood out. It didn't involve any city scene or even a broken floodwall. The painting showed a single, flood ravaged farmhouse. There was no sign of life. No people populated the scene, just the ruined, crumbling, flooded structure.

"Haunting, isn't it?" he asked, seeing Rachel's attention focus on the piece.

"Yes, it is," she agreed. "Do you think this painting is of a real farmhouse?"

"I would think so," he said after a pause.

"I would love to talk to the artist. Do you know who painted it? Did you paint it?"

Tanner looked surprised. He laughed loudly. "You think I painted them?"

"Well, they all deal with flooding and you seem obsessed with floodwalls and river flooding. It makes sense," she told him.

"Well, it's true I have some strong views about the misguided Corps of Engineers and the folly of trying to wall up rivers. But, Rachel, I am no painter."

"But you know who painted them?"

"Yeah. But I won't betray his confidence."

"Is Win his real name?"

"What do you think?"

"I don't think it's his real name."

"You are perceptive. I will give you that. Win is not his real name, but it does offer a clue. That's all I will tell you." Tanner invited her to the living room, where they both took seats on an antique, olive colored divan.

Rachel turned the conversation to Elroy's murder trial. "Aren't you angry that the defense attorney suggested you might have killed Billy?"

"Sure. That damn attorney blindsided me."

"So, can you give me any information that might demonstrate your innocence? I mean, Rush also questioned Harvey Winston."

"You said it."

"Do you think Harvey could have shot Billy? If so, do you have any evidence?"

"Rachel, you have the clues. You just need to follow them." Rachel looked perplexed.

"What clues?" she asked urgently. "What clues?"

"You've seen them."

Rachel tried to envision what he was talking about. Suddenly, it came to her. The paintings. Tanner was talking about the paintings.

"Win is the key," she said softly.

"You said it, not me."

"Win, Win, Win. Could it stand for Winston, as in Harvey Winston?" she asked.

"That's not for me to say," replied Tanner. "Like I said before, 'follow the clues.' By the way, he added, is your painting for sale? I'd love to buy it."

"No," said Rachel. "It's not for sale. I don't know why but it speaks to me."

"I knew it," cried out Tanner. "You see what I see. You see how floods can damage us. Your painting, my paintings, speak to that."

Rachel decided it was time to leave. She returned to the dining table and carefully rewrapped her artwork. She thanked him for showing her his paintings. Tanner walked her to the door. Once there, he opened the door and turned aside to let her pass as she carried her painting. His right hand briefly touched the small of her back, surprising her. She had no desire to linger. She hurried out the door and to her car parked in the driveway quickly placing the painting inside.

"We should talk again," Tanner called out.

"Maybe," she said even as she questioned if that was a good idea. But as she drove down the street, her focus had already turned to Harvey Winston. Those paintings might have just pointed her toward a murderer and someone who wanted to blow up the wall. That thought made her shiver.

CHAPTER THIRTY-EIGHT

Connor drank unsweet tea with two lemons as he listened to Rachel recount her meeting with Tanner. Rachel and Connor had decided to meet at Smooth Buns for breakfast the morning after her questioning of Tanner.

Both had ordered asiago cheese bagels with cream cheese. Rachel had her usual sweet tea. Connor hated sweet tea. It tasted like pure sugar to him. Once, driving through Georgia years ago, he had stopped at McDonald's for lunch. He had ordered tea, thinking it would be unsweet. What he got was sweet tea. He couldn't drink the stuff. It was horribly sweet. It made him want to throw up.

Rachel told Connor every detail of her meeting with Tanner, except for one. She didn't mention that Tanner briefly touched the small of her back as she was leaving. It wasn't like he touched her breast, but it still felt awkward to her. She wasn't sure how to take it. Was it intentional or just an accidental touch? She didn't know. Still, there was no need to tell Connor, she reasoned. She already had feelings for Connor. No need to add any more emotion into the situation.

"Wow," said Connor after Rachel finished talking. "So, Tanner is still trying to implicate Harvey."

"It looks that way. If Harvey did paint those eerie watercolors, we have to look at him as a serious suspect."

"Harvey never said anything about those paintings when I spoke to him."

"Yeah. But you didn't know about the paintings when you spoke to him. We need to talk to him, ask about the paintings."

"And we need to find out why Tanner has those paintings," said Connor. "Maybe Tanner and Harvey are working together. That would be smart. Each one placing suspicion on the other."

"You could be right. Maybe they are both playing us. But how are we going to find out?"

"The paintings could hold the key," Connor replied. "For one thing, they clearly show a tighter connection between the two men than what they let on."

"True. I think we need to show Harvey my painting. Maybe he'll open up a little more."

"Either that or he'll quit talking to us," worried Connor. "Still, we need to ask the questions."

Rachel nodded in agreement as she ate the last bite of her bagel. Connor called Harvey on his cellphone. The East Elmwood mayor had just come out of another meeting with the Corps commander and was in no mood to talk to the reporters. But he reluctantly agreed after Connor mentioned that Tanner had shown Rachel the paintings. Rachel and Connor met Harvey at the city park gazebo overlooking the downtown. The day was partly sunny and breezy.

"That damn Walsh. He's still bent on destroying my town just to save a bunch of rich Missouri merchants. It's downright evil," said Harvey after greeting Rachel and Connor.

"Is there anything you can do to stop him?" asked Rachel.

"The only thing the village can do is file a lawsuit and try to stop the demolition in the courts. I've been in touch with a lawyer. The suit should be filed today or tomorrow in federal court, but that's off the record until it's filed. Then, I'll be glad to talk to you."

"We'll hold you to that," said Connor. "Meanwhile, we have some questions about those paintings."

"Right. I'm surprised Tanner showed them to you. He's pretty private about his possessions."

"Well, I own one of the flood pieces," Rachel explained. "I recently bought the watercolor from Betsy's antique store." She carefully unwrapped the painting which she had placed against one of the concrete columns that supported the roof of the restored gazebo.

Harvey's eyes sparkled as he gazed at the painting. "Still looks pretty good," he observed, a look of accomplishment spreading across his face. "I haven't seen that painting in years."

"So, you did paint it and all the others?" asked Rachel.

"Yep. Tanner was telling you the truth. I guess I painted all of those about 10 years ago."

"You sold them to Tanner?" she asked.

"Yeah. I don't remember exactly when. I recall Tanner and I ran into each other on a street corner in downtown Elmwood. We talked about people we knew in East Elmwood. I mentioned I had taken up painting flood scenes. He was intrigued and asked to see them. I told him I would take photos of the pieces and email them to him, which I did."

"And when was this?" asked Connor.

"Oh, about seven years ago. He emailed me back and said he would buy all of them. At that point, I was no longer painting. I still collected guns. So, I sold the paintings. I won't tell you what he paid for them, but it was a good amount."

"How come you didn't sell Tanner the watercolor I just bought?" Rachel questioned.

"Because your painting was not actually part of the series. I painted this painting first. It was only later that I decided to create a series of flood paintings. The first painting I gave away to a friend in East Elmwood. I never imagined it would be worth anything."

"Betsy said she found it taped to the underside of a table she bought at an estate sale," Rachel said.

"My friend passed away recently. I had forgotten all about the painting," replied Harvey.

"But why would your friend hide the painting?" asked Rachel.

"I have no clue, but maybe he wanted to keep it from being discarded by relatives. After all, art is in the eye of the beholder. I hope you don't plan to hide it too," Harvey said.

"No, of course not. I plan to display it in my apartment. Not sure why, but I'm drawn to it."

"Well, I'm glad you appreciate it."

"Those paintings show a lot of anger," Connor observed, stepping into the conversation. "Were you trying to work out the anger you felt over Hamilton's death?"

"Maybe. But it was more than that. Over the years, I've seen the federal government repeatedly ignore the flooding concerns of the village. Congress has refused to fund construction of a concrete floodwall like Elmwood has. You know why? Because the Corps of Engineers doesn't think it's important to protect East Elmwood. From its perspective, East Elmwood is too little to worry about. So, what if we all drown?"

"That's harsh," said Rachel.

"It's the truth and, yes, it makes me angry."

"Angry enough to kill Billy and plot to blow up the floodwall?" questioned Connor.

An irritated look appeared on Harvey's worn, tired face. "I've told you I had nothing to do with Billy's death and I don't intend to dynamite the wall," he yelled. "Quit trying to pin this on me. It's Tanner you should be questioning. It's his uncle that died."

"We have," responded Connor. "He keeps pointing the finger at you. Maybe you both are working together, plotting to blow up the wall. That would explain why you are both pointing the finger at each other, trying to confuse us."

"You're crazy," shouted Harvey. "Stop badgering me. Leave me alone," he yelled as he turned and walked away.

"You pushed his buttons, Connor," said Rachel as she watched Harvey stomp off.

"Yeah. I have a tendency to do that."

"You sure do."

"I take that as a compliment," he remarked.

"You would," she said laughingly.

CHAPTER THIRTY-NINE

Harvey didn't bother telling Connor when the lawsuit was filed in federal court. His attorney did. Attorney Andy Dalton mid-week phoned Connor, who was plugging away on a story about the latest flood forecast. Heavy rains in the Upper Midwest had sent a ton of water racing downstream. The Mississippi River had climbed to within eight inches of the top of the aging floodwall. Emergency preparedness officials weren't sure if the wall would hold. They'd never seen the river this high.

Connor listened to Dalton relay the news: Harvey had scheduled a news conference for 11 a.m. on the closed-to-through-traffic Mississippi River bridge. Connor looked at the clock on his computer. It was 10 a.m. Nothing like a lot of notice, he thought. Still, he thanked Dalton. Personally, Connor liked Dalton who had a good reputation as a straight shooter with the news media. That wasn't the case with many lawyers, who viewed the media as some type of deadly virus. Most said as little as possible to reporters. Some of them refused to speak to reporters at all. Increasingly, many of the politically conservative attorneys in town and the public at large viewed news reports as "fake news," repeating the president's mantra. These days, anyone who didn't like a particular news story called it "fake news." It drove Connor crazy listening to such idiots.

When Connor and photographer Tyler showed up, the bridge was already crowded with news media, including reporters and videographers from television stations as far away as St. Louis. Harvey was talking to political leaders from both Illinois and Missouri. The East Elmwood mayor was dressed in khaki pants, a blue short-sleeve dress shirt and a dark blue tie. It wasn't Harvey's usual attire. Connor couldn't remember ever seeing him in anything, but jeans and T-shirts in the summer, jeans and plaid flannel shirts in the winter.

In the background, Connor could see the large pumps that ran constantly to funnel floodwater through massive hoses, sending it away from the village and back into the river downstream. In addition to the mayor and members of the village board, many of the town's beleaguered residents had shown up, boating across flooded streets or maneuvering through floodwater in tan and black rubber waders. Their haggard faces told the story. They were tired of combating the watery monster, navigating through flooded streets and yards, and climbing over sandbags to reach the relative safety of their homes and trailers. With no vehicular traffic on the bridge, Connor easily heard the constant hum of gas-powered pumps straining to keep the village from drowning.

Dalton, a 30-ish guy with black-framed glasses and wearing a gray suit, began the news conference. Speaking behind a microphone, he announced that on behalf of the mayor and village board he had filed a lawsuit in federal court that morning. The suit sought an injunction to block the Corps of Engineers from blowing up the earthen levee protecting the village.

Dalton then introduced Harvey, who took a moment to stare solemnly at the cameras. "We have taken our fight to federal court because Maj. Gen. Ted Walsh and the Army Corps of Engineers is not the least bit interested in saving our village. They only care about protecting the city of Elmwood across the river. And why is that? Simple, Elmwood has more people and more money, lots more money. Politically, East Elmwood is nobody. Why worry about a few hundred, largely poor residents? Well, I'm here to tell the Corps it's wrong. Our village board is unified. We will not sit by idly while the Ted Walshes of the world try to drown our town. Our attorney has asked for an expedited hearing to put a halt to the Corps-planned destruction. We know that our friends in Missouri don't want to see our village destroyed. We urge you to contact your congressional representatives and tell them to put the brakes on the Corps. We need common sense to prevail and right now that's in painfully short supply when it comes to the Corps of Engineers."

Harvey kept talking for another 10 minutes before introducing a special guest. Connor gasped with surprise when Harvey introduced the guest, announcing that this man knew all about the damage caused by blowing up an earthen levee. The guest was Demetrius Patterson, whose brother had drowned when the Corps of Engineers blew a huge hole in a Missouri levee south of Elmwood in 2011 to save the Illinois city of Cairo. The action wiped out the small, black community of Grassley.

Demetrius was dressed in blue jeans, a white dress shirt and new Nike shoes, not the grease-covered attire that marked his career as an auto mechanic. Connor looked to his right and saw Tyler snapping away, capturing all the action. Even before Demetrius started talking, Conner knew his speech would be powerful. Demetrius began by recounting all the actions of the Army Corps of Engineers leading up to the decision to blow the levee and flood thousands of acres of farmland and the tiny community of Grassley.

"No one consulted us," he told the crowd. "The way the Corps saw it, we were expendable. We had to leave our homes, our parents' homes, our community. Well, my brother Darius didn't get out in time. He drowned trying to flee in his pickup truck. As far as I'm concerned, the Corps killed my brother. They have blood on their hands and they'll do the same thing to East Elmwood if they get a chance. You have to stop them anyway you can," he said, raising his voice. "It's not just about lives. It's about community. We all had federal flood insurance. Guess what? After our small town was washed away, we found our flood insurance didn't cover manmade destruction. The insurance wouldn't pay us anything. It's crazy crap. The gov'ment can kill a town, especially an African-American place, and we don't get a dime. It's freakin' evil," he said, concluding the news conference.

Connor approached Harvey. "That was some news conference."

"Glad you liked it," Harvey said in a tone showing he was still irritated at Connor.

"I didn't know you knew Demetrius."

"Actually, I have you to thank for that, Connor."

"How so?"

"Don't you remember? Early on during the flood fight when you interviewed me, you mentioned having interviewed Demetrius. You told me how the black community had been wiped out by the big, bad Corps of Engineers."

"Ah, I did do that. I'd forgotten," Connor replied.

"Well, I'm sure we will see you in court."

"You can count on it, mayor. You can count on it." Connor eyed Demetrius who was walking west on the bridge. He hurried after him "Hey, Demetrius wait up."

Demetrius turned his head just as Connor caught up. "You still think I'd want to blow up the floodwall?"

"I was just asking questions when I spoke to you earlier. I wasn't insinuating anything."

"Well, you could have fooled me. What do you want?" asked Demetrius.

"I just want to ask, how did you come to be a part of this show?"

"Harvey contacted me. He asked and I said, 'yes.' It gave me a chance to tell the media what happened to Grassley and the wrong done to my brother."

"Well, you sure made your point. You might have found your second calling."

"As what?"

"A motivational speaker. Or maybe you should think about running for city council."

"I'm not sure Elmwood is ready for a black councilman," Demetrius said, shaking his head.

"Don't be so sure. This town is changing."

"Maybe not fast enough. But, regardless, when it comes to flood control, the real power resides with the Corps of Engineers. The decisions of Maj. Gen. Walsh and others like him determine if a community lives or dies."

"I'd like to think local residents and leaders have a say in their future," said Connor.

"You're dreaming," replied Demetrius, letting out a short laugh. He shook his head as he walked toward his vehicle parked on the Missouri side of the bridge.

Connor stood still, wondering just how futile it might be to fight the Corps of Engineers. And he thought about the anger that spewed forth from Demetrius, a man who clearly hated the Corps. But he also wondered about Harvey, who had made it clear he would do just about anything to protect East Elmwood. Would that include blowing up the floodwall, destroying downtown Elmwood to save his own village? Would it?

CHAPTER FORTY

Spectators and the news media crowded into the spacious, federal courtroom in Elmwood. People sat shoulder to shoulder on the benches, except for the very front benches on either side of the aisle. Reporters sat there. No one really wanted to sit next to them, which was fine with Connor. It gave him more room to spread out and made it easier to take notes.

The federal courtroom was a monument to government spending. The room featured mahogany paneling on the walls. The large desks for the attorneys were made of red oak. The judge's oak bench was massive, the front of it adorned with a bronze eagle. Behind him was the United States flag and the flag of Missouri. Even the jury box was luxurious, with cushioned chairs that would make anyone want to serve on a federal jury.

The courtroom was one of four courtrooms on the second floor of the three-story brick building, which featured a domed atrium in the marble-floored lobby. Security was tight as always. Everyone had to go through metal detectors. No one could bring their cell phones into the building, a major hassle for the news media.

Harvey was there, along with the entire village board. Maj. Gen. Walsh showed up too, dressed in his spotless military uniform. He was seated ramrod straight, staring straight ahead. Connor saw Tanner sitting in the back of the courtroom, taking it all in. Elmwood city officials were there too, including Elroy who made sure reporters saw him. Despite being accused of murder, Elroy wasn't taking a back seat to anyone.

Andy Dalton was seated at one of the attorney's tables, dressed in another of his many gray suits. At the other table sat Rush Johnson, representing the Corps of Engineers. Rush showed up in the best blue suit money could buy. This one came from a New York tailor. He wore a blue and red bowtie and black Italian leather shoes that were so polished they practically sparkled with every step he took.

"All rise," said the bailiff as Judge Archibald Halverson strode into the courtroom in his flowing, black robe. He took his seat on the bench and looked out at the eager crowd. Halverson was slightly overweight, in his late 50s and nearly bald.

He spoke quietly, but firmly. The judge was all business. "We are here in the case of the Village of East Elmwood vs. the United States Government, Army Corps of Engineers," he read from the case file on his computer screen.

After acknowledging the two attorneys, Halverson outlined the proceedings. Connor assumed the judge was doing so mostly to let the spectators know what was going on.

"Mr. Dalton, you filed the motion on behalf of your clients, Mayor Harvey Winston and the Village of East Elmwood in an effort to block the Corps of Engineers from detonating the East Elmwood agricultural levee. Is that right?"

"Yes, your Honor," said Dalton rising from his seat.

"Very well, you can proceed," said Halverson.

"Thank you, your Honor. My clients are seeking an injunction to stop the Army Corps of Engineers from blowing a hole in the earthen levee which is all that protects East Elmwood from the ravages of the Mississippi River."

The judge interrupted Dalton. "And why is the Corps wanting to blow the levee?"

"In an effort to protect the city of Elmwood because of concern the concrete floodwall could fail and/or be topped by the rising water," replied Dalton.

"I see," said the judge before urging Dalton to continue.

"Judge, it's our position that the Corps of Engineers is ignoring the devastation it would cause East Elmwood, a small community with limited financial resources. Even if the river flooded Elmwood's downtown, the city would be able to recover. The same can't be said for East Elmwood. It would wipe out the community. It would be destroyed forever."

"I've read your suit," Halverson told Dalton. "I want to hear what Mr. Johnson has to say."

Johnson rose and adjusted his bowtie. "Judge, I want to make it clear the Army Corps of Engineers has not decided to blow up the Illinois levee. The agency, however, is considering doing so, if necessary, to save Elmwood from massive destruction. It's a difficult decision, but the agency feels it must look at taking steps to protect Elmwood in the same way it chose to protect Cairo, Illinois, several years ago. The Corps of Engineers has made it clear to Mayor Winston that East Elmwood residents should start evacuating in case it becomes necessary to blow the levee."

The judge interrupted. "Is the Corps making preparations to open up the levee?"

"Yes. Liquid explosives have been loaded on a barge in Memphis. The barge should be here by tomorrow and then steps will be taken to put liquid explosives into pipes should a controlled explosion be necessary," Johnson said.

"And when does the Corps anticipate making a decision on whether to blow the levee or not?" Halverson asked.

"As soon as possible. Probably within a few days. Based on the river gauge today, the Corps may need to open the levee by early next week, if not sooner."

There were still more questions from the judge to both attorneys over the course of an hour, most of them dealing with the federal bureaucratic procedures needed for the agency to legally rip a hole in the levee.

At the end of the hearing, Halverson said he would take the matter under advisement and decide by the end of the day on whether to issue a temporary injunction. "But let me be clear," he added. "even if I issue a temporary injunction, it will still allow the Army Corps of Engineers to make preparations for blowing the levee. The agency, however, won't be allowed to carry out such action as long as the injunction stands."

Spectators spilled out of the courtroom. The crowd was mostly quiet, having seen a civil dispute play out in often confusing legal language. They had expected to see a heated debate but came away feeling cheated. Connor hurried past the parting crowd. He had a deadline to meet. He wanted to get the bulk of the story written while he waited to top the story with the judge's ruling.

The ruling came hours later, around 5 p.m. when Connor's stomach was growling. It seemed to Connor that news always broke when he was the hungriest. The judge had issued a temporary injunction, a partial victory for East Elmwood.

Harvey was working to fix a broken pump in East Elmwood when he heard the news from Dalton. He was relieved, but he knew it was just the first skirmish in the legal war. He desperately hoped river levels would drop, eliminating any thought the Corps had of blowing the levee. Otherwise, he thought, things might really explode. His mind focused on his flood paintings, the images of collapsing concrete and people drowning in downtown Elmwood. The bold colors flooded his brain, images full of anger and fear.

CHAPTER FORTY-ONE

Police Chief Blair Bonney got up to leave. The daily emergency preparedness meetings, held in a cramped conference room in the Corps of Engineers' temporary downtown headquarters, had become tiresome and repetitive. Bottom line, no one could be certain the wall would hold up or the river wouldn't top the wall. But all the river models predicted the crest would come soon, before Memorial Day. It couldn't come soon enough for emergency operations officials, including Blair. Maj. Gen. Walsh motioned for the police chief to stick around after the others left. He ushered Blair into his office and invited him to take a seat.

"I wanted to talk to you about Harvey," said Walsh.

"He was just at the meeting. What's up?"

"Well, I'm concerned he might try to damage the floodwall."

"Are you really concerned or are you just mad the mayor succeeded in getting a temporary injunction blocking your agency from blowing up the East Elmwood levee?" asked Blair.

"That's unfair."

"Is it? Or have you been talking to Connor?"

"No. You know I don't like talking to reporters that much. This lawsuit has turned into a circus. Everyone thinks we're the bad guy. Why did you ask me about Connor?"

"Because he's been acting like some ridiculous private eye. He believes the mayor is innocent of killing that bartender and that someone wants to destroy the Elmwood floodwall."

"Does he have any suspects?" asked Walsh.

"Yeah. One is Harvey and the other is this professor named Tanner Holloway."

"There you go," said Walsh, seizing on the comment. "Now you have another reason to keep an eye on Harvey."

"Not really. My top detective has interviewed both men and looked into Connor's suspicions. There's no evidence to show that either man has any intention to blow up the wall. And there's no evidence linking Harvey or Tanner to the murder of Billy Moss. The evidence shows the mayor killed his nephew."

"Well, do me a favor, keep an eye on Harvey for me. I think he would do anything to save his village, even something criminal," said Walsh.

"Very well. But I don't think you have anything to worry about with Harvey or, for that matter, Tanner. It's more likely the wall will be destroyed by the Mississippi rather than anything man would do to it," replied Blair.

"I'm worried about the river too. In my job, I have to prepare for everything," observed Walsh.

"You just worry about the river," advised Blair. "I will let you know if you need to worry about anything else."

***

Back at the newspaper office, Connor was doing some digging, looking into the possibility of a third suspect, Demetrius Patterson. Could he be angry enough about his brother's death to want to destroy the floodwall?

Demetrius had filed a federal civil suit against the Corps of Engineers over the death of his brother. The suit claimed his death was the direct result of the Army Corps' decision to blow up an agricultural levee, destroying the black community of Grassley. The suit sought $10 million in damages. The case lingered in federal court in Elmwood for years before a judge dismissed the case, siding with the agency which claimed no responsibility for the death of Demetrius' brother. The agency argued that Darius Patterson died because he failed to evacuate soon enough. Bottom line, the federal agency wasn't to blame. At least, that's how the judge had ruled.

Demetrius Patterson had denounced the ruling, telling reporters at the time that the judge "had blood on his hands." But would Demetrius have the know-how to plan a bombing? More to the point, did he have access to the necessary explosives? Connor realized he needed to know more about Demetrius.

At the same time, eight blocks south of the downtown, a man was carefully reading every word written about the temporary injunction. He knew from reading Connor's front-page story and watching the morning news that the Corps of Engineers had appealed the federal judge's ruling. But deep down, the legal battle made very little difference to him. The man knew what he had to do. No judge's ruling would keep him from his destiny.

The man gazed around his secret place, a rented garage off an alley in a rundown section of Elmwood. He had covered the windows with cardboard and transformed the interior into a workshop. A large workbench stood in the center of the building. Piled atop the table were sticks of dynamite, detonating cord and empty sandbags. He put aside the newspaper and made sure the only door to the building was locked. He powered up an old portable radio and tuned it to a classic rock station. Led Zeppelin's "Stairway to Heaven" rocked the airwaves. The man sang along.

The man carefully tied detonation cord around each stick of dynamite. As he moved along, he slowly and meticulously maneuvered several sticks of dynamite into each bag. He tied the cords snaking out of each bag to the main detonating cord. It took him nearly two hours to finish the job. He wasn't in a hurry. Better to take his time and do it right. He couldn't make a mistake, not now when he was so close to completing his mission.

Stored separately in the garage were blasting caps and safety fuses. He'd need them later to kick-start the demolition process. He liked to think he "borrowed" the materials even though he knew the stuff was stolen. But it wasn't like he could go and buy dynamite in his local hardware store. The man didn't think of himself as a criminal, not like someone who robbed a bank or raped a woman. His actions deserved praise, he believed.

He wiped sweat from his brow. The garage wasn't air conditioned and he had kept the windows closed out of secrecy. A fan sat in the corner blowing warm air on him. Earlier in the spring, the garage had been chilly. But the May weather was heating up. He opened a window just slightly, not enough for people to see in. Not that he figured anyone living in the neighborhood of worn-out houses and vacant buildings would care. And certainly, the police wouldn't pay attention to an aging garage on a largely abandoned alley.

He drank from his water bottle. The water was no longer cold, but it quenched his thirst. He pulled out a gray tarp and covered his handiwork stacked carefully on the workbench. No need to risk someone seeing it, although he figured his secret was safe. No reason to suspect anything. He had an eight-month lease and he had paid cash in advance. The landlord could care less about the place as long as he got his money.

In the background, the radio played "Hotel California." The Eagles tune resonated with him. The wall was his beast. He had to kill it. There was no other option.

CHAPTER FORTY-TWO

Harvey was nervous. Seated at his cluttered city hall desk, he listened to the steady hum of the pumps that were barely keeping the village of East Elmwood above water. He tried to calm his heart, which seemed ready to explode through his chest. He worried about making the call. A lot was riding on it. He sighed and picked up his cellphone and punched the number of Connor Tate.

"I've got something to tell you, but not over the phone," a nearly breathless Harvey told Connor. "Where are you now?"

"I'm walking in the downtown city park."

"Alone?"

"Yes, alone."

"Your girlfriend isn't there?"

"Who? Rachel?"

"Yeah."

"She's not my girlfriend," said Connor, his face turning slightly red. He didn't like people prying into his personal life. "Rachel isn't here. I haven't talked to her today."

"I'll meet you in the park. We'll take a walk, maybe feed the ducks," said Harvey, trying to quiet his breathing as he pictured the Elmwood floodwall exploding.

"I'm sure the ducks will love it," said Connor as he headed toward the pond. Twenty minutes after phoning Connor, Harvey showed up in a T-shirt, jeans and old tennis shoes. Bobo followed at his heels. Harvey greeted Connor at the pond as some ducks swam nearby, attracting Bobo's interest. The mayor appeared worried.

"What's wrong?" asked Connor as the two men sat on a park bench.

"I've seen the dynamite," he said breathlessly. "I found it in a run-down garage off an alley. It's all wired up."

"Slow down. Tell me what happened."

"I had been to a flood-update meeting at the Corps of Engineers office yesterday. I was heading home, driving down River Street

164

when I observed a man down by the floodwall. The man was inspecting the floodgate up close, running his hands over the gray wall and along the edge of the floodgate. No one else was around. The man was wearing a cap pulled down on his face and a large jacket which hung down to his knees. The man looked up and down the street a few times before heading to his vehicle, some type of SUV, dark in color. He drove away and I followed him."

"Now why did you do that? I know when I'm driving, I am focused on where I am headed, not what is happening off the roadway."

"I don't know why I followed him. I just did. Something about him didn't seem right."

"Did you recognize him?"

"No," responded Harvey, looking away. "The man drove in a seemingly random fashion, up one street and down another. He seemed to be doubling back at times as if unsure of where he was going."

"Or maybe it was just an effort to make sure no one was following him," suggested Connor.

"Could be. At any rate, he pulled into an alley and drove onto a weed strewn lot, parking behind a concrete-block garage. The man headed to the garage door, located at the back of the building and went inside. I pulled my pickup over to the edge of the alley, well back from the garage. The windows in the garage were covered with cardboard. He was in there about 10 or 15 minutes. Not long."

"You saw him leave?"

"Yep. He came out and drove away, headed down the alley. I waited to make sure he was gone and then got out of the truck and approached the back of the garage. The door was locked. There were no windowpanes in the door. I couldn't see in. So, I went around to the side of the building. There was a window, which had been opened a crack. I looked around to make sure no one was watching and then I slowly raised the window and climbed inside."

"You were taking a big chance. If you were spotted, you could have been arrested for breaking and entering," said Connor.

"Well, I don't know why I did it. I just did," said Harvey, sounding a little unsure of himself.

"What did you see? Was it just one big room?"

"Yep. I saw a tarp-covered workbench smack dab in the middle of the room. I was curious. I went over and pulled up one end of the gray tarp."

"And that's when you saw the dynamite?"

"Not at first. I saw the sandbags, but then I saw cord snaking out of each bag. Having worked at the quarry, I knew it was detonating cord. So, I looked inside one of the bags and saw the dynamite. I checked another bag and another. They were all packed with sticks of dynamite and all of them were connected together."

"Enough to blow a hole in the floodwall?"

"No doubt. It would make a big explosion."

"Did you look around some more?"

"No. I covered the bags of dynamite with the tarp, just like I found it. I then climbed through the window, shut it and ran to my truck. I wanted to get the heck out of there. I don't need police suspecting me of wanting to blow up the wall. I've already been questioned enough by you, Connor. And I'm no murderer. I didn't kill that bartender. I've told you that."

"You think that could be the same dynamite stolen from the quarry?"

"It has to be," replied Harvey. "There's no other explanation."

"You need to contact the police," said Connor.

"No, that's why I contacted you. If I go to the police, they might view me as a suspect. I thought maybe you could talk to the police and leave me out of it. Just tell them you heard about it from an anonymous source."

Connor remained quiet, mulling over the request. "Tell you what, I'll talk to my detective friend. I will try to keep your name out of it for now, but sooner or later if police find the explosives in the garage, they are going to want more information. Your name may come up."

"I understand," said Harvey, "but I appreciate it if you can keep me out of it. If this man is a mad bomber, I fear he might come after me."

"I think he'll have a lot more to worry about than you if police recover the explosives," Connor said. "And that needs to happen soon."

Harvey didn't have an address for the garage, but he gave a

good description of the place and how to get there. After he and Bobo retreated to the pickup truck, Connor phoned Adam on his cellphone, hoping his message would not go to voicemail.

Adam answered right away. Connor could hear noise in the background and then it died out. "You caught me mowing my lawn," said Adam. "What's up?"

"I have a lead on the stolen dynamite. I just can't tell you my source, but I can tell you where to find the dynamite."

"Hold on," said Adam, rushing into his house to grab pen and paper. He wrote down the directions he received from Connor.

"Can you check it out?" asked Connor.

"Yeah. I'm headed over there now. You can meet me there."

It took only 15 minutes for Connor to arrive at the alley garage. He waited another 15 minutes for Adam to arrive in his personal car, a four-door black Toyota. Adam wasn't in his usual suit-and-coat attire. He was wearing gray cargo shorts, blue polo shirt and blue Skechers.

Adam stepped out of his car and joined Connor who was standing on the edge of the alley, eyeing the garage. "Doesn't look like much," Adam said as he and Connor walked to the building. The first thing they noticed was the cardboard covering the few windows in the place.

"Looks like he didn't want prying eyes," Connor said.

"Yep. Looks that way to me too," agreed Adam as he and Connor walked carefully around the exterior of the garage, hoping to look through a window, but all were covered with cardboard, taped up from the inside. They returned to the dirt-stained door. Adam put his ear to the door. After a minute, he turned toward Connor. "No sound. I don't think there is anyone inside." Adam tried turning the rusty door handle, but it was locked.

"We could break in," suggested Connor.

"No way. We need to do this by the book. I'll need a search warrant to get a look inside this place."

"You think a judge will grant one?"

"If I can get the right judge to accept the little information that I have," said Adam. "Basically, I have you telling me that a third party told you he saw the dynamite after breaking into the building after following some guy for no particular reason. I'll see what I can do.

167

Maybe the judge will buy it."

Adam walked toward his car. "I need to check some real estate records and see who owns this building. I suspect, judging from its run-down appearance, it's a rental. Any search warrant will have to be served on the landlord or we will need to get the owner's permission to search the place.

"Good luck," said Connor. "Keep me posted."

"I'll let you know," said Adam.

Connor watched Adam drive off. He was tempted to try and enter the building through the unlocked window that Harvey had mentioned, but he resisted. Adam was right. It needed to be a legal search. It was mid-afternoon when Connor received a text from Adam. "Good to go," it read. Connor called Adam. He wanted to hear the whole story.

"Judge Fisher signed off on the search warrant although he made it clear he thought the request was pretty flimsy," the detective told him.

"I'm surprised you found him at home?"

"I didn't. He was playing golf with the police chief. I had to drive a golf cart over to the ninth hole to get the damn thing signed. Of course, I had to explain the situation to Blair too."

"What did Bare Bones say?"

"He agreed with the judge. He thinks it's a pretty weak case for a search, particularly since you were the one who gave me the tip. He had some choice words for you. Still, the chief doesn't want us to ignore a report about possible stolen dynamite."

"Did you find out who owns the place?" asked Connor, ignoring the "choice words" comment.

"Yes. County records show it is owned by some guy in California. I managed to get his contact number. I called him. When I explained the situation, he agreed to let us look inside after I sent him a cellphone photo of the search warrant."

"Do you have a key?"

"He keeps a spare key with a friend of his who lives in Elmwood. I went over and picked up the key."

Adam and Connor agreed to meet in 30 minutes at the garage. Connor didn't tell Adam he had informed Rachel of the situation. She wanted to tag along and he couldn't blame her.

Connor picked up Rachel in the River City Journal parking lot. Neither talked much as they drove to the garage. They both were eager for the hunt. Adam was waiting by the garage door when they arrived. He stiffened a little when he saw Rachel. He was friends with Connor, but he barely knew Rachel beyond the fact that she worked for the newspaper.

"You guys stay here while I check out the place," he told them. "I don't want you messing up the evidence."

Connor and Rachel nodded in agreement. Adam put the key in the lock and opened the door. He walked inside. The space smelled of bleach. The whole garage looked spotless and totally empty. No tarp, no dynamite, no nothing. The scene shocked Rachel and Connor. They stepped inside and gazed at the space.

"I can't believe it," said Connor. "This isn't what I was told."

"Maybe he was spooked, decided to clear out the place," Rachel suggested. "From the smell, it appears he wiped the place clean."

"Seems to be the case. Maybe he doesn't need the place anymore. Maybe he's ready to use the dynamite," Adam said.

"That's a scary thought," replied Connor.

"Looks like another dead end," sighed Rachel.

"I wouldn't say that," said Adam, drawing a surprised look from both Connor and Rachel. "We know who rented the place."

"And who is that?" asked Connor.

"Harvey Winston."

"That can't be," said Connor.

"Why, because Harvey told you about the dynamite?" asked Adam. The look in Connor's eyes told Adam all he needed to know even as Connor sought to answer him.

"I didn't say that."

"You don't have to. Your eyes gave it away. You'd never make a good poker player."

Rachel chimed in. "But if Harvey rented the garage, why would he keep that a secret? Why would he make up a whole story about finding dynamite? And Harvey said a man entered the garage. The man would have had to have a key. None of this makes any sense."

"Harvey would have a key if he rented the place. Maybe he just wanted to mess with you Connor. Maybe he made the whole thing up," said Adam. "Or maybe he just wants you to think that. Maybe he stole the dynamite, but later felt guilty about it. Wanted to confide in someone, but then changed his mind, decided to move the dynamite. Whatever the story, I think Mr. Winston has some major explaining to do."

CHAPTER FORTY-THREE

Fear knifed through the man's heart. Sweat covered his brow. An hour earlier, he had returned to the garage, his quiet hideaway. He entered as he always did. It was a hot and humid May day, more fitting of late June. The masonry block building felt like a kiln. It needed ventilation. He turned toward the one window he previously had cracked open. Something was wrong. He knew it right away. The window looked closed. He approached it as if were a deadly virus. Bending down, he stared at it. The window was shut. He was certain he had left it open a crack. Now it was completely closed.

Fear hit him like a fastball. Someone had closed the window. He rushed to the workbench and lifted the tarp. The dynamite was still there. But now he was worried. Why would someone close the window? The answer took his breath away. No one would have closed the window unless he or she had first climbed through it and then exited the same way. The man returned to the workbench. He removed the entire tarp and studied the bags filled with sticks of dynamite linked together with detonation cord. He tried to remember how he had left them. He spotted a stick of dynamite resting partly out of a bag. He was sure he hadn't left it that way. He was too particular to have packed the bag so carelessly.

Someone had seen the dynamite. The police might show up any minute, he worried. The man knew what he had to do. He had to move the stuff, and right away. He carried the bagged explosives to his SUV, along with blasting caps and fuses, and extra detonation cord. He dragged the wooden bench across the concrete floor. He turned it on its side to get it through the doorway. Then he dragged it across the weedy ground to his vehicle. He maneuvered the table onto its end and leaned it against the rear bumper. His back muscles ached. He lifted the end of the workbench and pushed it onto the rear floor of the SUV and slid it in. It barely fit. He slammed the rear door shut and turned around in all directions to see if he had been observed. He saw no one and breathed a little easier. Still, he felt his heart pounding.

He rushed back into the rented garage and looked around. In the far corner, he spotted the plastic container of bleach and an old towel. He had stored them so he could wipe down the interior when he no longer needed the place. He just hadn't planned to do it so soon. He grabbed the bleach and the towel and began wiping every surface: windows, walls and even the floor. He took down the cardboard and wiped it off before carefully taping it back on the windows. Then he wiped them again, making sure he cleaned the tape too. When he reached the door, he carefully cleaned it with bleach. He poured bleach over the door handle too and wiped it with the towel. Then using the towel, he opened the door and walked out. He closed it, locked it and cleaned it from top to bottom with bleach. He then thoroughly soaked the outside door handle with bleach before wiping it down.

Satisfied, he carried the bleach and towel to his vehicle and placed them on the front passenger-side floor. Once safely inside the vehicle, the man locked the doors. He sat there; his clothes drenched in sweat. It took him a few minutes to realize he hadn't started the vehicle. He turned the key and the engine hummed. He turned the air conditioning to full blast. He needed to cool down. He drove home like a little old lady, driving slower than the speed limit and constantly glancing around as if someone knew he was hauling stolen dynamite. He was so flustered, he pulled into a convenience store parking lot at one point just to catch his breath. He was relieved when he finally made it home. Maybe he was safe now. Still, he worried, the police might already suspect him. What if they came to his door?

The man shook his head, trying to remove the worries and, more importantly, the fear. He walked to the kitchen and opened a cabinet. He took out a bottle of bourbon and poured himself a glass. He didn't bother cutting it with water. He drank it in a single gulp, absorbing the liquid's familiar burn. He had to pull himself together. He knew that. Everything depended on it. He couldn't wait much longer. He couldn't risk it. It was time for things to go boom.

***

Connor waited impatiently throughout the rest of the day to hear back from Adam. It was well into the evening before Adam phoned. He had spent hours interviewing Harvey at the police station. Harvey had not been arrested, just questioned.

"Harvey kept telling me he didn't rent the place. I learned from the landlord that his friend in town, Peter Finch, handled the renting of the place. Finch told me that some guy left a typed note in his mailbox seeking to rent the place. He included a name and a cellphone number. He called the number and the guy identified himself as Harvey Winston. Finch told him he could rent the place. The man said he would pay the rent in advance in cash and leave it in Finch's mailbox. After receiving the cash, Mr. Finch deposited it in his bank account and then made an electronic payment into the landlord's account in California. Finch left the key to the garage in the mailbox and the man apparently picked it up. Finch said he never saw the guy and never drove by the garage. I figure the man made the transaction late at night when everyone was asleep."

"Can you trace the phone number?" Connor asked.

"No. The guy must have used a burner phone, one of those prepaid phones you can buy at Walmart. You use it and then throw it away."

"So, did Harvey rent the garage?"

"I don't know. He denies it. He sounds sincere, but I know he often has a lot of cash around. He admitted as much to me after I discovered Harvey is a minority owner of Club Mardi Gras."

"What?"

"Yeah. Harvey pockets thousands of dollars in cash from the club every week. He told me it's his share of the profits. Sometimes he has it in his house for several weeks before he deposits it in a bank in Elmwood. There are no banks in East Elmwood."

"So, he could easily have paid the cash to rent the garage," Connor said.

"That's the way I see it."

"But why would Harvey tell me about the dynamite if he was planning to blow up the wall?"

"That is strange. It doesn't make sense."

"Unless Harvey is looking to confuse us," suggested Connor. "Maybe he wants us to believe someone else intends to dynamite that wall. Maybe he and that someone, possibly Tanner, are working together to destroy the wall."

"That could be the case," agreed Adam. "If so, maybe the dynamite was never in the garage. We only have Harvey's word about the dynamite. He could be playing us."

"Harvey repeatedly has suggested Tanner could be the culprit. Tanner implied Harvey fits the bill as the would-be bomber," said Connor. "It makes sense if they are plotting together. Of course, there could be another suspect."

"Another suspect?"

"Yes. Demetrius Patterson. He blames the Corps of Engineers for the drowning death of his brother in the 2011 flood," Connor said.

"Do you really think he is a solid suspect?"

"I'm not sure. He lives on the city's southside, only about a block away from the garage where Harvey said the dynamite was stored. But as far as I can tell, Demetrius never worked at the quarry. I don't think he knows the first thing about explosives."

"Still, anyone can find a lot of information on the internet about how to use explosives. A person could teach himself how to use dynamite," observed Adam.

"You have a point, but I still think Harvey and/or Tanner are more likely suspects. So, where does that leave us?"

"Without anyone to arrest," said Adam.

"What about Tanner?" asked Connor.

"We can't arrest Tanner for stealing dynamite when we can't find the explosives. Besides, I think Harvey is hiding something."

"What makes you say that?"

"He told you and later told me that he couldn't identify the man he was following. But Harvey knows Tanner. If it was Tanner who he trailed, why didn't he identify him?"

"I don't know. Maybe he just wanted the police to confiscate the dynamite. Maybe he was protecting Tanner, didn't want to see him arrested," Connor speculated.

"But if Harvey doesn't want Tanner arrested, why suggest Tanner might want to destroy the wall? I'm not convinced Tanner has any role in this. There's no evidence putting him near the dynamite or implicating him in Billy's murder," said Adam. "His opposition to floodwalls seems philosophical, not criminal."

"I don't know about that," replied Connor. "I told you about all those eerie flood paintings Tanner has."

"Yeah. Well, last time I checked, having strange paintings is not a crime, and certainly not grounds for a search warrant," Adam said. "Besides, Harvey painted them. That sure makes him a better suspect in my mind."

After their chat ended, Connor punched in Rachel's number on his phone.

"You're calling rather late," she said.

"It's only 10 p.m."

"Well, I was kind of tired. I was thinking of going to bed."

"Change of plans. We need to talk."

"Pillow talk?" she asked, her tone lighthearted. Her comment made him smile.

"No," he said, recounting his conversation with Adam and the detective's view that Harvey, not Tanner, is a more likely suspect.

"So, you want to meet and talk about it?" she asked.

"Yes. I think that would be best."

"Well, let me put something better on. I'm wearing sweatpants and an old T-shirt right now."

"I'm sure you look great."

"Thanks, Connor. But you haven't seen me without makeup."

"I'll meet you at Alligator Alley in half an hour," said Connor.

"Make it an hour and you've got a date," she said cheerfully.

"Deal," said Connor. After their conversation ended, Connor went into his bathroom to splash on cologne. The mirror reflected his smile.

CHAPTER FORTY-FOUR

Conner camped out at one of the restaurant's back tables waiting for Rachel to arrive. He ordered a Blue Moon and watched the crowd of mostly young people, college kids, kicking back and enjoying themselves on a Saturday night. Some of them looked like they already had drunk a little too much.

He spotted Rachel moving through the crowd congregated at the bar. She was wearing skinny black jeans, a turquoise short-sleeve blouse and black leather sandals. She wore a turquoise bracelet on her left wrist and a simple silver ring on her right hand. Her hair flowed loosely down her back. It was still wet. She had taken a quick shower before getting dressed. She saw Connor and smiled. She walked over and sat down across from him.

"Thanks for the invite," she said, her sparkling eyes trained on him. There were questions in those eyes, he knew, and they just didn't deal with Tanner Holloway. She ordered a glass of Chardonnay. They made small talk until the waitress brought her drink.

"I wanted to talk to you about Tanner," Connor said. "We need to keep tabs on him."

"Can't the police do that?" she asked.

"No. Adam made it clear, they aren't watching him. They don't think the college professor is a murderer and they certainly don't believe he has any plans to dynamite the wall."

"I was beginning to think Harvey was the most likely suspect. After all, his village would benefit most from the destruction of the floodwall," she said.

"I was too. But I can't believe he would have told me about finding the dynamite in that run-down garage if he wanted to blow up the wall," said Connor. "Adam's convinced Harvey is the more likely suspect, but what if he's wrong?"

"So, that leaves Tanner," she said. "Of course, it's possible we are totally off base, and Tanner is innocent. That would leave Harvey."

"Or someone else, maybe Demetrius Patterson. He blames the Corps of Engineers for his brother's death. He's carrying around a lot of anger."

"Enough to kill?"

"Maybe so, but as far as I can tell he never worked at the quarry and never handled explosives."

"So, you still see Tanner as a likely suspect?"

"I do."

"I agree," said Rachel. "His fixation with all those paintings seems odd. When I was at his house, I got the feeling he was struggling to control his emotions. He wanted me to think everything was under control, that he wasn't some crazy dude."

"We need to stake out his house, not all day, just late at night. If he's going to attempt to bomb the wall, he'll do it in the cover of darkness."

"I think you're right. I figure any attempt would come after midnight, likely closer to daybreak," said Rachel. "By then, even the drunks would be off the downtown streets. There would be less chance he'd be seen."

"We only need to stake out his house for those hours after midnight," Connor advised, drawing a nod of agreement from Rachel.

"When do you want to begin this undercover work?" she eagerly asked.

"Tomorrow night. I don't think he'd try anything tonight. He'd wait until tomorrow. Most of the downtown stores are closed on Sunday and the restaurants and drinking establishments close earlier."

"Makes sense," she said, but Connor could see she was trying to figure something out.

"I see that look. What is it?" he asked.

"I wonder if he would wait a few more days. The river is supposed to crest Tuesday. If I were wanting to blow up the wall, I would wait until it crested or just before it did."

"If you're right, that means the attempt might not occur until Tuesday. Either way, we only have to do this stakeout for a few days. He's bound to make a move by then."

"Should we tell Lansmon what we're doing?" she asked.

"No way. He'd just tell us to quit trying to be detectives. He might even order us not to do it. I don't want to risk that. It's better if we keep him out of the loop for now."

"What happens if Tanner does try to detonate the explosives? How are we going to stop him? We're not the police."

"I can't answer that. I haven't worked that out."

"So, you're flying by the seat of your pants as always," she said, letting out a merry laugh.

"You got a better idea?" he asked, cracking a broad smile.

"No. I'm just along for the ride and, as I see it, it could get bumpy."

They finished their drinks and their discussion of a stakeout. Connor paid the bill, but neither got up to leave. They sat there, both watching the crowd, neither of them uttering a word. The silence was uncomfortable, but both were unwilling to break it. Finally, Rachel spoke up. "As long as we are out tonight, you want to go listen to some music?"

"Sure," said Connor, relieved by her suggestion. "Jello?"

"Jello it is," she said, quickly getting to her feet. Connor joined her and they moved outside into the clear, breezy night air. They walked the several blocks to the jazz bar. Halfway there, walking side by side, their fingers met and they held hands the rest of the way. Rachel and Connor heard the soulful sax sounds before they even entered the club. The House band, "Soul Shades," was in the middle of another set. A tattooed waitress with red-dyed, close cropped hair showed them to a table. They ordered a bottle of California Merlot and soon were sipping their drinks and listening to the music.

The band played a Billie Holliday classic, "You Go to My Head." A 20-something, tan woman, wearing a sparkling gold dress cut low in the front and high on the legs, sang the tune. The song ended and the band rolled into the next tune, Nat King Cole's "Unforgettable." Several couples took to the dance floor. Rachel and Connor joined them. Connor pulled her close and she wrapped her right arm around his left shoulder. He put his arm around her waist. Neither spoke. She moved her head close to his and looked up into his eyes. He felt her hair on his cheek.

Rachel's lips moved to his and she kissed him, slow and soft. He kissed her back as they continued to dance. Their embrace lasted longer than the song. The other couples had left the dance floor.

They looked up, somewhat embarrassed, and returned to their table.

They sat down and both quickly drank more wine. An hour later, they had danced a lot more and finished the bottle. Connor paid the bill. She insisted on leaving the tip. They walked back to their vehicles parked in one of the downtown surface lots. Hand in hand, they walked to her car. She unlocked it before turning around. Pulling him close, she kissed him long and slow. He responded, eagerly kissing her, feeling the warmth of her body against his. As quickly as it began, Rachel pulled away. She cast an inviting smile at Connor before climbing into her Mini Cooper. She rolled down the window and he bent down and kissed her again. "See you, Connor," she said. "We need to do this again."

"Soon, I hope," replied Connor.

"I'd like that," said Rachel, brushing back strands of hair from her face in the breezy night air.

CHAPTER FORTY-FIVE

The man woke up in a sweat. He sat up wide eyed in bed, looking around his bedroom, trying to bring his mind into focus. He must have imagined it, the police coming to his door. His mind cleared and he realized he'd been dreaming. Still, it made him fearful. He couldn't wait any longer, he needed to move the dynamite into place.

The man looked at the clock on his bedside table. It read 4 a.m., a perfect time to get ready. He dressed and ran a comb through his graying hair. Black was his color: Long-sleeve shirt, jeans, socks and even shoes. Everything was black, the better to hide his actions in the early morning darkness. He entered the garage and mentally made a check list to make sure everything was stored in his SUV. At 4:30 a.m. on Sunday, he opened the garage door and backed slowly out of his driveway. He glanced up and down his street. There were no lights on in the neighboring houses. Everyone was asleep.

He was relieved there was very little traffic. He drove slowly, staying within the speed limit and looking out for possible cop cars. He didn't want to draw anyone's attention, particularly the cops. Twenty minutes later, he arrived at his destination and backed into an on-street parking spot near the floodwall gate. He sat still for about five minutes, checking to make sure no one was around. The area was quiet. Even the street corner nearest the floodgate was empty. Hours earlier, it would have been filled with people leaving the bars, and someone would have been playing a guitar on the street corner for tips. But now, there was pure silence. Even the drunks were in bed.

He stepped out of his vehicle and eyed the floodgate. City crews had placed rows of filled sandbags against the bottom of the gate to prevent seepage. Extra, filled sandbags were stacked in front of the wall abutting the edge of the gate. The man opened the SUV's rear door and began hauling dynamite-filled bags across the 20-foot-wide grassy strip of land to the edge of the floodgate. It took him 20 minutes to get all the bags moved up to the wall, staying as close to

180

the ground as possible. He carefully removed some of the city's extra sandbags from the pile and replaced them with his dynamite-filled bags. With the aid of a small flashlight, he checked to make sure the detonation cords were in place. Satisfied, he piled the city sandbags on top, further hiding the bags of explosives.

He looked around, checking to make sure he hadn't been seen. He saw no one. The riverfront was eerily quiet. Even the raging river was silent. He returned to his vehicle, closed the rear door and climbed into the driver's seat. He started the vehicle, the engine breaking the dark silence. The man put the vehicle in gear and drove away. He wanted to speed, to hurry home. But he took his time, driving five miles below the speed limit. He stopped at every traffic signal and made sure he signaled at every turn. A siren sounded in the distance. His heart pounded. He listened for it to come closer, but the sound faded away. He decided it was an ambulance rushing someone to the hospital. He finally made it home. He pulled into the garage. Only after he had closed the garage door did he breathe a sigh of relief. Everything was ready to go boom. The thought made him smile. Once inside, he walked to the kitchen, opened the fridge and grabbed a beer. His nerves felt on fire. He could barely contain his excitement. He sat at the kitchen table until the sun came up, reliving every aspect of the dark trip.

Fog greeted the Sunday dawn before giving way to a bright blue sky adorned with the occasional tapestry of white clouds. Connor woke up early, took a hot shower and dressed. He left the house in blue jeans, a T-shirt and blue Skechers. It was chilly at 7 a.m., so he took along a jacket. He drove to the city park overlooking Elmwood's downtown and parked the vehicle. The lot was empty. He followed the paved trail through the park. A woman, probably in her 30s, jogged past him trying to hold onto her youth. He moved to a park bench at the eastern end of the park. From there, the downtown spread out below him. He eyed the wall. The swollen Mississippi River stood within inches of the top of the concrete wall. He saw the sandbags neatly stacked in front of the floodgate and by the wall. There were a lot of bags there, more than he previously remembered. But then the pile of sandbags, Connor knew, typically grew over the course of a flood fight as the city added to the stockpile.

The sun was higher in the morning sky now. Connor walked

back to his vehicle. He drove downtown, parking in front of Smooth Buns, one of the few businesses that kept Sunday hours. Oliver opened the bakery and restaurant promptly at 8 a.m. Connor was the first customer.

"How are you doing, Connor?" asked Oliver, who sported a well-worn Ohio State University sweatshirt, old jeans and New Balance all-terrain shoes that had seen better days.

"Okay. Wish this flood was over," said Connor.

"You and me both."

"What's good today?"

"Everything, of course," said Truman as he joined the conversation. Truman was dressed in designer black jeans, a pink, long-sleeve shirt and polished loafers. After some good-natured bantering, Conner ordered scrambled eggs with Colby cheese, bacon strips and an Asiago cheese bagel, bread sliced. He usually drank unsweet tea, but he was in the mood for coffee. He ordered a cup of Hazelnut coffee. When the food came, Oliver and Truman joined him at the table, eager for news of the reporter's investigation.

"So, what have you found out?" asked Oliver.

"Do you think that East Elmwood mayor killed Billy and plotted to blow up the wall?" asked Truman.

"I was beginning to think so," said Connor. "But now I am not so sure, even though the police see him as the most likely suspect. Even then, they don't put much stock in the idea that anyone is really going to attempt to blow up the wall. As for the murder, the police and the prosecutor still think Elroy killed Billy."

"But you don't think so," said Oliver.

"No. I believe the person who shot Billy intends to bomb the floodwall with dynamite stolen from the quarry."

"Do you have another suspect?" asked Truman.

"Tanner Holloway."

"The professor dude?" questioned Truman.

"Yes, that guy. The floodwall seems a personal affront to him," said Connor. "But Harvey has motive too. Maybe both of them are involved. I don't know."

"Well, I hope you can figure it out. We don't want the flood to drown our establishment," said Oliver, his face creased with worry.

"At least, the river is expected to crest in a few days and then things may start getting better," Truman observed.

"But the water will go down slowly. It will likely remain above flood stage for another month," Connor pointed out. "Still, I think the crest is key. If anyone intends to dynamite the wall, it probably would occur around the time the river crests. So, something has to give in the next few days."

"Well, you better eat your breakfast," said Oliver. "Sounds like you're going to need to fuel that mind of yours to solve this mystery."

"You're right about that," said Connor. "Besides, it's a delicious breakfast."

Several blocks away, Harvey sat in his well-rusted pickup truck parked on River Street. Bobo, comfortably at home in the passenger seat, eyed Harvey like only a true companion can. Harvey petted Bobo and gave him a doggie treat. Harvey had had a restless night after having been grilled for nearly two hours earlier that day at the Elmwood police station. How dare they accuse him of stealing the dynamite and plotting to blow up the floodwall, he thought. That detective, Adam Dade, seemed intent on making him out as a criminal.

Just thinking about it made Harvey angry. Still, he knew he had to calm down, couldn't let the police get under his skin. He hadn't been arrested. That was a good thing. As a result, he could still do what he had planned. A day earlier, sitting in an interview room at the station, he had worried the police would arrest him. He didn't think any charge would stick, but it would have played havoc with his plan. Harvey eyed the floodwall as he smoked yet another cigarette.

He kept gazing at the sandbags piled against the wall abutting the closed floodgate. He thought about just scrapping the whole thing but decided against it. This time he had no choice, he had to succeed. Not just for himself, but for Tanner. Bobo stirred. He was ready to go home. And so was Harvey. Nothing could be accomplished in broad daylight. He'd need the cover of darkness. For now, he would just hurry up and wait.

CHAPTER FORTY-SIX

Late Sunday night, Connor steered his Ford Escape onto Tanner's street and parked a block from the professor's house, close enough to keep an eye on it, but not too close. He opened his driver's side window a little to let in the cool night air and turned off the engine. Two blocks away a dog barked, but Tanner's neighborhood was quiet. There were no lights on. Everyone was in bed, Connor presumed.

He hoped he wasn't betting on the wrong horse. Maybe he should be staking out Harvey, not Tanner. But the flooding in East Elmwood would have made it challenging to do so. People would notice a strange vehicle waiting around on a flooded street. Deep down, he suspected Tanner. Or was it just that he liked Harvey, didn't want to believe the East Elmwood mayor could be a mad bomber. The clock on his cellphone told him it was midnight. He figured he had some time to kill. He doubted Tanner would make a move before 2 a.m., maybe later Monday. But Connor didn't want to take a chance. He had come prepared for a lengthy stakeout. He had packed a can of Coke, a bottle of water, Oreo cookies and beef jerky. He also brought his pillow. He lowered his seatback slightly and placed the pillow behind his head. From this angle, he could still see Tanner's house just fine. Just in case he fell asleep, he set his phone alarm to beep every hour. But for now, Connor was wide awake. He had taken a nap Sunday afternoon in preparation for the task at hand. He took a sip of the soft drink and chewed on beef jerky. An hour into the stakeout, his phone rang. In the quiet of his SUV, the noise was alarming. He answered.

"Hi," greeted Rachel.

"What are you doing up?"

"I couldn't sleep. I kept thinking about the stakeout. Is everything okay?"

"Yeah. Everything's dead here."

"Well, call me if Tanner makes a move."

"I will, but you should get some sleep, Rachel. No need for both of us to stay awake."

"Okay. But promise me you'll be careful."

"You can count on it," he said even as he wondered what he'd do if Tanner pulled a gun on him. He prayed it wouldn't come to that.

He had just finished his conversation when he spotted a light in a small window of Tanner's house. It stayed on only a few minutes and then the space went dark again. Connor figured Tanner had gone to the bathroom and then back to bed. By 3 a.m., Connor was singing songs to himself in an effort to stay awake. Images of Rachel danced through his brain. At 3:30 a.m., he turned the key just enough to engage the battery and turned on the SiriusXM radio in his vehicle. He didn't want to run down the battery, but he needed to stay awake. He tuned to a Classic Rock station. The Eagles were singing. "Take It Easy." He quietly sang along.

By 5:30 a.m., pre-dawn light was starting to define the landscape. The sun would be rising soon. Connor concluded Tanner wouldn't take a chance now. Still, he waited around another half hour. Lights came on in the house next door. Still more lights shined across the street. People were waking up. Time to go home. Connor didn't want people seeing his vehicle parked on the street. He started the vehicle, shifted it into gear and drove home. He was tired and disappointed. There was nothing to show for his effort except an empty Coke, a partially empty bottle of water and a meal of cookies and beef jerky. Not much to write home about or write anything about. What was Tanner waiting for? An even bigger question rattled in his brain. What if Tanner didn't kill Billy and isn't planning to blow up the wall? What then? Connor had no answers.

It was 10 a.m. before Connor showed up in the newsroom. He had taken nearly a three-hour nap. He spent much of the last hour nourishing himself with cups of black coffee in an effort to secure an energy boost. Lansmon greeted him by telling him that he looked "terrible." Connor grunted and collapsed into his desk chair. Lansmon simply smiled and walked back into his office. He knew better than to try to carry on a conversation with Connor right then. He figured Connor needed more time to return to the living.

Rachel stopped by Connor's desk. "You look…"

"Don't say it."

"Terrible," she finished.

"Yeah. I heard that from Lansmon."

"You think Tanner will make his move tonight?" she asked.

"He has to do it tonight," Connor said, sighing loudly. "The river is expected to crest tomorrow. I can't see him waiting much longer."

"Unless we are all wrong and no one plans to blow up the wall."

"I can't believe that," said Connor.

"Or won't believe it."

"That too," he said as Rachel walked back to her desk. An hour later, he felt better. He was back with the living. Then Harvey called him.

"Bad news," Harvey told him. "A federal appeals court in St. Louis just overturned the injunction."

"The Corps of Engineers can blow up your levee?"

"Yep. That's what it means. Our attorney is appealing to the U.S. Supreme Court for an emergency stay of the order, but it's doubtful the justices will take it up. Ted Walsh called me. They plan to blow up the East Elmwood levee Tuesday morning, around 8 a.m. They're telling everyone in East Elmwood to evacuate before they drown our town."

"I'm sorry, Harvey," said Connor. "Is there any way to stop it short of Supreme Court action?"

"I've spoken to the Illinois governor and he has appealed to the state's congressional delegation in Washington. He hopes they can stop it. I'll let you know if I hear anything," Harvey said before ending the conversation.

Connor turned to Rachel. "It's back on. The Corps plans to drown East Elmwood tomorrow."

"Oh, my God," said Rachel. "What a disaster."

Connor turned back to his desk and began making phone calls to Maj. Gen. Walsh and local emergency officials on both sides of the river. He even called Elroy, seeking a comment from the beleaguered Elmwood mayor, who lamented plans to demolish any levee. Within half an hour, he had typed up a "breaking news" story and the newspaper posted it online. By late afternoon, East Elmwood was largely a ghost town. Only Harvey and a few others including

186

strip club owner Marissa Hue remained. The rest packed up what belongings they could and moved out, urged on by the Illinois State Police, the Corps of Engineers and emergency officials.

Then the story changed. Harvey called Connor with some unexpected good news. Thanks to political pressure from the Illinois governor and that state's congressional delegation, the commanding general of the Army Corps of Engineers halted plans to detonate the East Elmwood levee.

"Thank God," said Harvey as he finished explaining the decision.

"I guess the commanding general decided the political fallout from wiping out a small town would be horrendous," Connor said.

"And Congress might have cut the agency's budget," said Harvey. "When it comes to government, Connor, always follow the money."

"Well, I'm glad the Corps of Engineers won't destroy your levee," said Connor. "But I bet Maj. Gen. Walsh wasn't too happy."

"No, I think he was really convinced the levee needed to go. From what I have observed, he doesn't like being second guessed even by those higher in command."

Connor thanked Harvey for calling and got back to work rewriting his story with the updated information. The story was quickly posted under the headline: "A Change of Heart: Feds halt plan to blow up levee." By 6 p.m., Connor readied to go home. It had been a long day and emotionally draining. He touched base with Rachel. "You up for the stakeout tonight?"

"Sure. You think Tanner will make a move now that the Corps won't be blowing up the East Elmwood levee?"

"I think Tanner still wants to blow up the floodwall. It's not just about saving East Elmwood. I believe he wants revenge for the drowning death of his uncle. Deep down, I think it's always been about revenge."

"Well, I guess, we'll see," said Rachel, who increasingly doubted Connor's belief. "I still wonder about Harvey."

"But now that the Corps has scrapped plans to destroy the East Elmwood levee, I think there is no longer a reason for Harvey to blow up the floodwall."

"Maybe. But it could be all about revenge for Harvey too," suggested Rachel. "He was close to Hamilton Jones and lamented the man's drowning."

"True. But the police already view Harvey as a more likely bomber. He knows that. Police don't suspect Tanner at all. If Harvey and Tanner are working together, it makes sense that Tanner would have to detonate the dynamite. It would be too risky for Harvey to do it."

"I hope you're right," said Rachel.

"Call me if Tanner makes a move," said Connor. "And, Rachel, be careful. If Tanner killed Billy, he might not hesitate to shoot anyone else who gets in his way."

"Don't worry. I'll be smart about it. I won't put myself in harm's way," she said. But as Connor walked out of the newsroom, he wondered if he was putting her in danger. The thought scared him. He wasn't used to worrying about someone else. He wasn't used to relying on someone else either. It made him uneasy.

CHAPTER FORTY-SEVEN

Rachel pulled her Mini Cooper to the curb, a half block away from Tanner's house shortly after midnight. She turned the motor off and looked around. The neighborhood of tidy, brick homes near the college campus was quiet. She scrolled through her song list on her cell phone and selected a sultry jazz tune. It calmed her nerves. Deep down, she hoped Tanner wouldn't leave his house. She was afraid of what might happen.

She took a deep breath and grabbed her Yeti mug of sweet tea. She drank the soothing drink. An hour later she was munching on an oats and honey granola bar. The only lights in the neighborhood were a few front porch lights. Three blocks in either direction, street-lights shined on the other side of the street. They cast shadows onto the roadway. Rachel's car was parked on the dark side of the street. As far as she could tell, no one was up.

By 2 a.m. Tuesday, she was starting to nod off. She turned to classic rock to keep herself awake. She scrolled through her playlist and selected Journey's, "Any Way You Want It," turning the volume up on her cellphone. Thirty minutes later, she almost screamed when Connor knocked on her driver's side window. She hadn't seen him approaching. He ran around to the passenger door.

She unlocked it and he slid into the seat. "What the hell are you doing here?" she asked, clearly surprised by his sudden appearance. "You about scared me to death."

"Sorry. I thought you would see me in your review mirror."

"I wasn't looking. I never figured on someone approaching me like that in the middle of the night. And, where is your car?"

"I parked on a side street about a block away. I thought it might be suspicious if someone in the neighborhood saw two cars parked together."

"You never answered my question. What are you doing here?"

"I thought I'd come and keep you company," said Connor.

"I appreciate that," said a now calmer Rachel. She noticed he

189

had changed clothes. He wore a seemingly new pair of blue jeans, a long-sleeve tartan plaid red and black shirt and black Converse shoes. Connor observed Rachel's attire. She looked gorgeous as ever, he thought. She was dressed in skinny jeans, a V-necked sea foam green blouse and a pair of Vans shoes, canvas tan in color. Her autumn hair was braided. Even in the dark, her eyes sparkled, Connor thought. Deep down, Rachel was glad Connor had shown up. It would make it easier to pass the time. Still, she didn't want him to think she couldn't handle a stakeout.

"You know I could have done this by myself," she said, turning toward Connor.

"I know. I couldn't sleep. I figured I might as well join you. If Tanner does make a move, you won't have to call me. So, it makes sense for us to do this together," he said with a grin. Rachel smiled back in an approving way. They spent the next two hours talking mostly about music, everything from jazz to rock songs. At 4:30 a.m., a light went on in Tanner's house, then another light. A shadow moved inside. Tanner was up. Connor and Rachel tensed up, their eyes laser focused on the house. Twenty minutes later, the garage door opened, and Tanner backed out his black Toyota RAV 4. He punched the remote, closing the garage door, and steered east toward downtown Elmwood.

Rachel waited until Tanner's vehicle was far down the street before she pulled her car into the driving lane and slowly followed him. Tanner drove way under the speed limit. "Why is he driving so slowly?" Rachel wondered aloud.

"Probably because he doesn't want to get pulled over by the cops," said Connor. "He's just being careful."

It was past 5 a.m. when Tanner pulled onto River Street. Rachel turned onto Main Street and clicked off her car's headlights. She made a sharp turn into a downtown alley, shut off the engine and coasted along a little farther before putting on the brakes. The alley emptied onto River Street south of the floodgate. Rachel and Connor quietly emerged from the car and walked as softly as they could toward the riverfront. They reached the end of the alley and peered around the corner. They saw a shadow near the floodwall. He was bending over, reaching into the sandbags. They gazed at him, their eyes adjusting to the darkness. They saw the stooping man more clearly. Shocked looks crossed their faces. It was Harvey. Was he the madman? Was he preparing to blow up the wall? But where was Tanner? Was he an accomplice? Suddenly, they spotted a moving shadow. It was Tanner, sprinting toward the wall and the sandbags.

"The dynamite must be there," Connor said. "Call Adam. Tell him to get down here. I've got to stop them before everything blows up."

"Be careful," said Rachel, kissing him on the mouth and holding him tight in her arms for a few seconds. Then Connor was gone, sprinting across the street and dropping to the ground as soon as he hit the grass.

Tanner looked back toward the street as did Harvey. Both men thought they heard the sound of someone running. They feverishly glanced up and down the street but saw no one. Connor was face planted in the grass, holding his breath, hoping he wouldn't be seen. Tanner's gaze returned to the wall and Harvey.

"What are you doing here, Harvey?" Tanner growled.

"I'm trying to save you."

"I don't need saving."

"I think you do. You brought me into this when you planted the can of paint in my office, trying to make it look like I painted that message on the floodwall."

"Yeah. I thought it was a nice touch. The worst part was having to pour red paint all over my car. But I hoped it would deflect attention away from me."

"It's not too late to put an end to this."

"Don't you see, I am ending it, ending this damn wall. Help me blow it up."

"I can't," said Harvey.

"Then get out of the way," yelled Tanner as he charged Harvey, propelling him backward. Harvey's head slammed into the concrete wall. His body went limp. Tanner quickly turned to the dynamite. Everything still seemed in place. He hurriedly unrolled the trunk line of the detonation cord and connected the fuse. He was shaken and angry. Harvey shouldn't have come. If only he had stayed away. He had no right to interfere. He should have been thrilled.

Tanner was helping East Elmwood and avenging Hamilton's death. Why didn't Harvey understand?

Connor had seen the scuffle as he crawled across the grass, his clothes getting wet from the dew. He moved within eight feet of Tanner who had his back to him. Suddenly, Connor saw a flame shoot out from Tanner's right hand. He had a long-neck butane lighter. He was going to ignite the fuse. Connor sprang from the grass as Tanner turned toward him. Surprised, Tanner dropped the lighter; the flame flickered out. Connor reached into his right pocket for the digital recorder. He turned it on.

"Stay away, Conner. This isn't your business. Let me do what needs to be done," shouted Tanner.

"You don't want to do this. You could kill lots of people."

"You mean like they killed my uncle?"

"A flood killed Hamilton Jones," said Connor.

"No, what killed him was this damn wall. It restricted the river, leading to bigger and bigger floods. Hamilton didn't have a chance."

"Billy Moss didn't have a chance. You shot him and then framed Elroy for the murder."

"You got it all figured out, don't you?"

"Pretty much," shot back Connor. "You stole the quarry dynamite. You've been planning this for months. But Harvey suspected what you were planning to do. He found the dynamite in that rented garage. But he didn't want you arrested."

"You're right about that. Me and Harvey were almost like brothers."

"But you didn't have to kill Billy."

"I couldn't take the chance he might have recognized me when he spotted me carrying the paint can after I painted the message on the floodwall. I was in Alligator Alley a lot. I was pretty sure he recognized me, maybe not at first. But the more police questioned him, the more he thought about it. By the time I shot him, I knew he had recognized me. It would have been only a matter of time until he told the police, only a matter of time until they ruined my chance for justice. I couldn't risk it."

"You shot Billy with your uncle's Colt pistol and then placed it in Elroy's office where you were sure the police would find it."

"You do make a good detective, Connor. I hadn't planned to kill Billy. Not at first. But then I was eating in the restaurant when Elroy barged in and threatened to kill Billy. For me, it was a stroke of good luck, a chance to silence Billy and shift the blame to Elroy, who deserved it."

"Why?"

"Because as mayor, he constantly went on about the merits of the wall, how it had saved Elmwood's downtown from countless floods. All the while, East Elmwood residents had to cope with ever-growing risks from larger and larger floods because of the wrong-headed policies of the Corps of Engineers. The Feds were killing the town I grew up in. Don't you see? I couldn't let that happen."

"But the Corps has pulled the plug on blowing up the East Elmwood levee. The town is safe. You don't need to do this," pleaded Connor.

"No. It's not safe as long as the floodwall stands. If not this year, then next year or the year after or the year after that a larger flood will come along and wash away the village. I won't let that happen," said Tanner, bending down to pick up the lighter. Connor lunged at him, knocking Tanner to the ground. Tanner kicked Connor in the chest, knocking him backward. Tanner reached for the lighter, his fingers grasping it. Then Connor was upon him, peeling back his fingers. The lighter fell to the ground. Sirens sounded in the distance. Connor knew the police were on their way. Tanner did too. He punched Connor in the face and kicked him in the groin. Connor doubled over in pain, but still managed to grab the lighter.

Flashing lights and screaming sirens grew closer. Tanner ran by the floodgate and jumped as high as he could, barely catching the lowest rung of the metal ladder permanently affixed to the wall. He climbed to the top of the wall. His head felt like it would explode; his months of planning ruined. All he could think about now was fleeing. He looked down and saw Connor racing toward the ladder. Connor jumped, but missed the ladder and fell to the ground. On his second try, his hands latched onto the lowest rung and he achingly pulled himself up. Tanner kicked at Connor's left shoulder, trying to dislodge him from the ladder. In doing so, Tanner nearly lost his balance. Connor held onto the ladder with his right hand and with his left hand pulled himself atop the wall, only inches above the racing floodwaters.

Tanner raced southward along the top of the concrete wall. Conner ran after him. Tanner's left foot slipped as he ran, plunging into the river. He pulled his foot back onto the wall, regaining his balance. But the slip allowed Connor to catch up. Connor tackled Tanner and the two men rolled over. Tanner's hands reached for Connor's throat. Connor slammed his right elbow into Tanner's nose, drawing blood. Tanner punched Connor in the face. Connor kicked back as Tanner tried to stand up. Losing his balance, Tanner fell backwards into the roiling river.

Connor plunged his right hand beneath the water, grabbing one of Tanner's flailing arms to pull him back to safety, but the current was too swift. In an instant, the river ripped Tanner from Connor's grip. The river rushed Tanner downstream as he struggled to stay afloat.

Branches in the muddy water bruised his face. He swallowed some water. The current was pulling him down. He slipped under. Desperately, he swam for the surface, his muscles screaming in pain. Then he broke through. He gasped for air. He was alive. He heard a loud swoosh. Something was near him. Tanner turned his head in the direction of the sound. He barely had time to make out the dark object, a massive log. It struck Tanner square in the head, cracking his skull. He cried out in pain. He slipped below the surface. He tried to breathe, but his lungs were filling with water. As he was dying, he saw his uncle, dressed in overalls, reaching a long arm out to him, pulling him into the watery darkness.

CHAPTER FORTY-EIGHT

Sprawled atop the floodwall, inches from the racing water, Connor breathed heavily, his heart pounding like a marching band drum. He tried to calm himself, turning his eyes away from the monster river. He had never seen a man drown before. It was horrible. He heard his name being called. "Connor, Connor." He looked down and saw Adam, Glock drawn. "Are you okay? Where's Tanner?"

"I'm okay," he sighed. "Tanner's dead. He tried to flee atop the floodwall. I tackled him and we struggled. He lost his balance and fell into the river. I reached out to grab him, but the current was too swift. It swept him away. He went under. Then he surfaced but was struck in the head by a log and sank below the surface. I never saw him again."

"It's tough to see a man drown, but better him than you," said Adam. "You need to come down. You look like shit."

"Nice to see you too," said Connor, struggling to turn his body around. Once headed in the right direction, he crawled along the wall to the metal ladder, then turned again and slowly descended. He reached the bottom rung, still seven feet off the ground, and hung there for a second before letting go. He landed stiffly. His legs buckled and he began falling backward. At that moment, Adam's sure arms reached out and embraced him, keeping him upright. "Thanks," mumbled Connor. Rachel grabbed his hand, concern racing across her eyes. His neck was badly bruised. One eyelid was swollen. His shirt torn. His pants scraped. His muscles ached.

"You look a mess," she said.

"Thanks. Adam told me the same thing. You guys really know how to make a guy feel good."

"Remember, I told you to be careful," said Adam. "You should have waited for the cavalry."

"Yeah. Well, you guys are a little late," said Connor, gazing at the police officers milling around the base of the wall, tending to the injured Harvey and inspecting the dynamite and bagging the evidence. "Is Harvey okay? You know he tried to stop Tanner."

"Yes. Harvey will be fine, but he'll have one hell of a headache. He's lucky. He could have been killed."

"It was never about blowing up the wall for Harvey," said Connor. "He was just trying to protect Tanner. They were like brothers."

"You should have left law enforcement to the police. You didn't have to be a hero," said Adam.

"Tanner was trying to light the fuse. I had to stop him. I couldn't let him blow a hole in the wall and send floodwaters crashing through the downtown."

"Did he tell you anything before he died?"

"He told me everything. He admitted to stealing the dynamite, killing Billy, framing Elroy and plotting to blow up the wall. It was all about revenge. He blamed the wall for the death of his uncle years ago. That rage ate away at him, I guess."

"I wish we could have arrested him, had a chance to interview him and get a taped confession," Adam lamented.

Connor fished in his right pocket, hoping the device was still there and hadn't fallen into the river or been smashed during the struggle. His hand found the slender device. It felt as solid as ever. Relieved, he looked Adam straight in the eyes. "I guess this is your lucky day," he said, pulling out the digital recorder and handing it to him.

"You recorded the conversation?"

"You bet. I think the prosecutor is going to want to drop the murder charge against Elroy after he hears this," said Connor.

"You know, you might just make a good detective," remarked Adam.

"I think I'll stick to being a reporter."

"Probably a good idea," said Adam. "There's too much bureaucratic paperwork for you. Plus, you'd have to carry a gun."

"Yeah, that's not for me."

Rachel put her arm around Connor's waist. "Come on, hero. Let me take you home," she said. He nodded and they began walking toward the alley and her car. "I hope you're not going to make a practice of doing this," she said with a smile. "So far, our dates have been a lot of shop talk."

"Don't forget tonight's stakeout," he reminded her.

"No, this one will be hard to top."

"I'll try to do better next time."

"I'm counting on it," said Rachel.

The rest of the week flew by. Connor wrote a lengthy front-page article about the murder, the events surrounding it and Tanner's plot to blow up the wall. Rachel wrote a sidebar about her visit to Tanner's home and the eerie flood paintings created by Harvey. Their stories were the most read articles the paper had experienced for months. The prosecutor dismissed the charge against Elroy, who celebrated with his supporters at Alligator Alley.

On Saturday, Connor and Rachel met for breakfast at Smooth Buns. Connor showed up in his best pair of blue jeans. He wore a red T-shirt and tan Skechers. Rachel came in ankle-tight jeans, a tie-died T-shirt of greens and golds, and sandals. She wore a neutral shade of glossy lipstick. Her auburn hair flowed down her back. They sat at a corner table. The place was packed. Some people came and went, picking up take-out breakfasts. Others stood around outside, waiting for a table to open up. Oliver and Truman greeted Rachel and Connor at their table.

"How are things going?" asked Oliver.

"Just fine," said Rachel.

Truman gazed at the bruises on Connor's neck and face. They were beginning to fade. "How do you feel?" he asked.

"Still sore, but getting better every day," said Connor.

"Glad to hear it," Truman said. Oliver nodded in agreement.

"We'd love to chat more," said Oliver, "but the place is a little busy."

"More like a lot busy," said Truman, "Just the way we like it," he added before he and Oliver headed off to check on other customers' orders.

When their waitress came over, Rachel and Connor both ordered spinach and artichoke souffles. They each had a glass of water, and they drank their share of mimosas. All in all, a fine start to a late May weekend. They spotted Harvey who had stopped in to pick up two asiago cheese bagels, bread sliced, with cream cheese. He stopped by their table as he was getting ready to leave with his bagged order.

"I want to thank you," he told them. "Without your efforts, people might have thought I was the villain."

"You mean if the dynamite had detonated?" asked Connor.

"Yep. I know the police cleared me, but that doesn't mean the public would have. Suspicions die hard around here."

"What made you show up at the floodwall?"

"Tanner called me after the Corps got approval to blow up the East Elmwood levee. He told me not to worry, that he would save the village."

"Did he explain what he meant?" asked Connor.

"No, but I knew what he was going to do. I knew the crest was coming. I figured that's when he would act. I guessed he would do it shortly before dawn."

"But you didn't tell the police."

"No. I thought I could talk him out of it. Maybe it was foolish on my part, but I had to try. You have to remember; I knew him before he became crazy with anger. I thought I could save him from himself. Besides, I never figured him for a murderer. I was so sure he didn't kill Billy. The Tanner I once knew never would have killed anyone. It's hard to fathom what goes through a man's mind to allow him to commit murder."

"I heard you inherited all of Tanner's paintings," Rachel said, breaking into the conversation.

"Can you believe it? The son of a bitch left me the paintings in his will."

"What are you going to do with them?" asked Connor.

"I may sell them again. An art gallery owner in St. Louis found out about the paintings. He called me asking if I might want to display and sell them at his gallery. I haven't decided for sure, but I think I'll say, 'yes.'"

"Wow, you're a regular Picasso," replied Connor. "Who knew?"

"Maybe you should paint again," suggested Rachel. "Something besides floods," she added.

"I might just do that now that East Elmwood is starting to dry out. The river level has dropped some. It's still way above flood stage, but the pumps are keeping up, and the repaired levee is holding."

"That's great news," said Rachel.

Harvey nodded and stood up to leave. "See you guys. Bobo's

in the pickup. He loves bagels. I'm sure he's drooling right now. I think we'll take a drive in the country. I want to enjoy the day. I know Bobo will."

"Hope your truck makes it," said Connor, a wry smile cracking his face.

"It may not look like much, being rusty and all, but that truck will go anywhere, kind of like me," he said with a laugh as he left. Harvey passed Elroy, who was coming in the door. The two mayors briefly acknowledged each other before going their separate ways.

Elroy showed up to pick up his two-quiche order. But he wasn't in a hurry. He stopped to shake hands with every customer, patting some of them on the shoulders and shaking hands with others. Still others, he greeted with hugs. Elroy was the mayor and he made sure you didn't forget it. When he made it to their table, he sat down to chat.

"I want to thank you guys for proving I didn't have anything to do with killing Billy," he said, his voice etched with emotion.

"We just did our jobs," said Connor. "It's what a free press does."

"Well, you know I've not always been a fan of the media, but I do appreciate what you all did. I just never really thought Tanner would do something like that, killing Billy and plotting to blow up the wall. I guess you never know what a person might do if they carry around feelings of revenge for years. It eats away at your soul. I think that's what happened to Tanner."

"Well, it certainly consumed him," said Rachel.

"I've been consumed with something else," said Elroy. "I've been thinking about Billy a lot. It would be nice to erect an outdoor sculpture in his honor."

"Something modern, no doubt," observed Connor.

"Yes. And one of these days, Connor, you'll come to appreciate such art."

"It may be a long time before that happens."

"You never know," said Elroy with a laugh as he rose to leave.

As Elroy left the restaurant, Connor spied Henry Carter and Marissa Hue sitting at a table across the room. He rose, walked over and greeted them. "I didn't know you knew each other," said Connor.

"Marissa has been a major donor to the museum," said Henry.

"What can I say, I like history and Henry knows a hell of a lot of it," she said.

"So, I guess with the water receding, your place will be back up and running soon."

"Yes. Club Mardi Gras will be hopping very soon. My girls will be back at work in East Elmwood. I'm glad for them."

"And for your bank account," replied Connor.

"That too. By the way, you should stop by sometime."

"I'm a little busy these days," said Connor.

"I see that," observed Marissa with a sly smile, gesturing toward Rachel.

"If you talk to her, put in a good word for me," Connor said with a wink.

"I'll do my best. But the invitation still holds, with or without your date."

"Thanks," said Connor, retreating to his table. Rachel looked inquiringly at him as he sat down. "She invited me to the strip club," he told her.

"Connor, you told her no, right?"

"Not exactly. I just thanked her, didn't want to hurt her feelings."

"Well, I think you should worry about my feelings more."

"I certainly do, which is why I think we should go out on another date."

"What type of date?" asked Rachel, her eyes eagerly watching him.

"A real date."

"Without all that cloak and dagger stuff?" she questioned.

"Something like that. No shoptalk. Maybe we could see a movie?"

"Why don't you come over to my place for dinner."

"What's on the menu?" he asked.

"I'll whip something up," said Rachel, her radiant, hazel eyes inviting to him. "Hope you'll leave some room for dessert."

"I definitely could embrace that."

"Oh, I think you will," she said with an engaging smile. "In fact, I'm counting on it."

The End

Made in the USA
Monee, IL
10 January 2022

88522283R00115